ERLE STANLEY GARDNER

- Cited by the *Guinness Book of World Records* as the #1 bestselling writer of all time!

- Author of more than 150 clever, authentic, and sophisticated mystery novels!

- Creator of the amazing Perry Mason, the savvy Della Street, and dynamite detective Paul Drake!

- THE ONLY AUTHOR WHO OUTSELLS AGATHA CHRISTIE, HAROLD ROBBINS, BARBARA CARTLAND, AND LOUIS L'AMOUR *COMBINED!*

Why?

Because he writes the best, most fascinating whodunits of all!

You'll want to read every one of them, from
BALLANTINE BOOKS

Also by Erle Stanley Gardner
Published by Ballantine Books:

The Case of the
COUNTERFEIT EYE

Erle Stanley Gardner

BALLANTINE BOOKS • NEW YORK

ISBN 0-345-33195-8

This edition published by arrangement with William Morrow and Company, Inc.

Manufactured in the United States of America

First Ballantine Books Edition: December 1986
Fifth Printing: February 1991

CAST OF CHARACTERS

PERRY MASON TURNED HIS BACK TO THE MORNING SUNLIGHT which streaked in through the windows of his private office and regarded the pile of unanswered mail with a frown.

"I hate this office routine," he said.

Della Street, his secretary, glanced up at him with eyes that contained a glint of amusement in their cool, steady depths. Her smile was tolerant.

"I presume," she said, "having just emerged from one murder case, you'd like another."

"Not necessarily a murder case," he told her, "but a good fight in front of a jury. I like dramatic murder trials, where the prosecution explodes an unexpected bomb under me, and, while I'm whirling through the air, I try to figure how I'm going to light on my feet when I come down. . . . What about this chap with the glass eye?"

"Mr. Peter Brunold," she said. "He's waiting for you in the outer office. I told him you'd probably delegate his case to an assistant. He said he'd either see you or no one."

"What does he look like?"

"He's about forty, with lots of black, curly hair. He has an air of distinction about him and he looks as though he'd suffered. He's the type of man you'd pick for a poet. There's something peculiar in his expression, a soulful, sensitive something. You'll like him, but he's the type that would make business for you, if you ask me—a romantic dreamer who would commit an emotional murder if he felt circumstances required him to do it."

"You can readily detect the glass eye?" Mason inquired.

"I can't detect it at all," she said, shaking her head. "I always thought I could tell an artificial eye as far as I could see one, but I'd never know there was anything wrong with Mr. Brunold's eye."

"Just what was it he told you about his eye?"

"He said he had a complete set of eyes—one for morning—one for evening—one slightly bloodshot—one . . ."

Perry Mason smacked his fist against his palm. His eyes glinted.

"Take away that bunch of mail, Della," he commanded, "and send in the man with the glass eye. I've fought will contests, tried suits for slander, libel, alienation of affections, and personal injuries, but I'm darned if I've ever had a case involving a glass eye, and this is going to be where I begin. Send him in."

Della Street smiled, vanished silently through the door which led to the reception room where clients who were to see Perry Mason personally were asked to wait. A moment later the door opened.

"Mr. Peter Brunold," she said, standing very slim and erect in the doorway.

Brunold marched past her, strode across the office to Perry Mason, thrust out his hand.

"Thanks for seeing me personally," he said.

The lawyer shook hands, stared curiously at Brunold's eyes.

"Know which one it is?" Brunold asked.

As Mason shook his head, Brunold smiled, sat down and leaned forward.

"I know you're busy. I'm going to get down to brass tacks. I've given your secretary my name, address, occupation, and all the rest of it, so I won't bother with that now.

"I'm going to begin at the beginning and give you the whole business. I won't take much of your time. Do you know anything about glass eyes?"

Perry Mason shook his head.

"All right, I'll tell you something. Making a glass eye is an art. There aren't over thirteen or fourteen people in the United States who can make them. A good glass eye can't be distinguished from a natural eye, if the socket isn't damaged."

Mason, watching him closely, said, "You're moving both eyes."

"Of course I'm moving both eyes. My eye socket wasn't injured. I've got about ninety per cent of natural motion.

"Now then," he went on, "a man's eyes vary. His pupils are smaller during the day than at night. Sometimes his good eye gets bloodshot. Lots of things may account for that, a long drive in an automobile, losing sleep or getting drunk. With me it's usually getting drunk. I'm sensitive about my eye. I'm telling you about it because you're my lawyer. I've got to tell my lawyer the truth, otherwise I'd see you in hell before I told you anything about having a bum eye. None of my closest friends know it.

"I've got a set of half a dozen eyes—duplicates for some, and some for wear under different conditions. I had one eye that was made bloodshot. It was a swell job. I used it when I'd been out on a binge the night before."

The lawyer slowly nodded. "Go on," he said.

"Someone stole it and left a counterfeit in its place."

"How do you know?"

Brunold snorted. "How *would* I know?" he exclaimed. "The same way I'd know anything. How would you know if someone stole your dog, or your horse, and left a cur or an old plug in its place?"

He took a case from his pocket, turned back the flaps and disclosed four artificial eyes in leather pockets.

"Carry that with you all the time?" Mason inquired curiously.

"No. Sometimes I slip an extra eye in my vest pocket. I've got a vest pocket lined with chamois skin, so the eye won't scratch. I always keep this leather case in my grip if I'm traveling, or on my dresser if I'm not."

He extracted a glass eye and handed it to the lawyer.

Mason held it in his palm, stared at it thoughtfully.

"Rather a neat job," he said.

"Nothing of the sort," Brunold contradicted. "It's a rotten job. The pupil's a little out of shape. The thing they call the iris is irregular; the colors aren't blended, and the veins are too red. A good vein for a bloodshot eye has a yellowish tint to it . . . Now, take a look at this eye and you can see what a good eye is like. Of course, that isn't a bloodshot eye like that first one I gave you, but it's an eye made by an expert. You can see the difference. It's got better color. The blending is better. The pupil is regular."

Mason, inspecting the two eyes, nodded thoughtfully.

"This isn't your eye?" he asked, tapping the bloodshot eye with his forefinger.

"No."

"Where did you find it?"

"In that leather case of mine."

"You mean to say," the lawyer asked, "that the person who stole your bloodshot eye took it from this case and put the counterfeit eye in the pocket from which the original had been taken?"

"That's right."

"What possible object would anyone have in doing that?"

"That's what I want to know. That's what I'm here to find out."

The lawyer raised a quizzical eyebrow.

"*Here* to find out?" he asked.

Brunold narrowed his lids until they were mere slits. He lowered his voice and said, "Suppose someone stole that eye in order to get me in bad?"

"Just what do you mean?"

"An eye is an individual thing. Very few people have exactly the same colored eyes. Artificial eyes, when they're well made, are as distinctive in style of workmanship as an artist's painting. You know what I mean. Half a dozen artists may paint a tree. All of the paintings will look like the tree, but there'll be something distinctive about each one that will show what artist painted it."

"Go on," the lawyer said, "tell me the rest of it."

"Suppose," Brunold said, "someone who wanted to get me in bad stole one of my eyes and left me a counterfeit? Suppose a crime was committed—a burglary, or, perhaps, a murder, and my eye was left at the scene of the crime? I'd have one hell of a time explaining to the police that I wasn't there."

"You think the police could identify your eye?" the lawyer inquired.

"Sure; they could if they went about it in the right way. An eye expert could tell who the man was that made the eye. He'd recognize the type of workmanship. The police could get in touch with that man and show him the eye. That fellow makes eyes for me right along. He'd take one look at it and say, 'Pete Brunold, 3902 Washington Street.'"

The lawyer's eyes were intent in their steady scrutiny.

"Do you think," he asked slowly, "that your eye is going to be left at the scene of a murder?"

Brunold hesitated a minute, then nodded slowly.

"And you want me to fix that?" the lawyer asked.

Brunold nodded again.

"A murder," asked Perry Mason, "of which you are innocent, or of which you are guilty?"

"Innocent."

"How do I know that?"

"You've got to take my word for it."

"And what do you want me to do?"

"Show me some scheme by which I can beat the rap. You're a criminal lawyer. You know the way the police work. You know the way juries think. You know the way detectives work up a case."

Mason swung slowly back and forth in his big swivel chair.

"Has this murder been committed?" he asked. "Or is it going to be committed?"

"I don't know."

"Is it," Mason asked, "worth fifteen hundred dollars to you to work a trick that will put you in the clear?"

Brunold said slowly, "That depends on how good the trick is."

"I think it's good," Mason told him.

"It's got to be better than good. It's got to be perfect."

"I think it's perfect."

Brunold shook his head and said, "There isn't any perfect scheme. I've gone over it time and time again in my mind. I stayed awake half the night trying to figure out some solution. There isn't any. That eye can be identified, if the police go about it the way I said. Understand, it isn't only a question of proving I'm innocent *after* the eye is identified. It's a question of *not wanting to have the police identify the eye.*"

Mason pursed his lips, nodded slowly. "I think I understand," he said.

Brunold took fifteen one-hundred-dollar bills from his wallet and spread them on Perry Mason's desk.

"There's fifteen hundred bucks," he said. "Now, what's the stunt?"

Mason handed Brunold the bloodshot eye, dropped the other in his pocket, picked up the bills and folded them together.

"If," he said slowly, "the police should find your eye *first*, they'll look it up and identify it in the way that you mention. If they find some other eye first, they'll try to identify that. If they find another eye second, they'll try to identify that. If they find your eye third, they'll take it for granted that it's just like the first two."

Brunold blinked his eyes rapidly. "Give that to me again," he said.

Mason said slowly, "You'll find out what I mean if you think it over long enough. The trouble with your eye is that it's too good a job. It's a work of art. You know that, because you know something about glass eyes. The police won't know that, not unless something happens to direct it to their attention."

Sudden animation lit Brunold's face.

"You mean," he asked, "that you're . . . ?"

His voice trailed away into silence.

Mason nodded.

"That," he said, "is *exactly* what I mean. That's why I fixed the price at fifteen hundred dollars. I'll have some expense in connection with the matter."

Brunold said, "Perhaps I could save some . . ."

"You," Perry Mason told him, "aren't going to know a single damn thing about it."

Brunold shot forth his hand, clasped the lawyer's hand and pumped it up and down.

"Brother," he announced, "you're clever! You're clever as the very devil. That's an idea that had never occurred to me, and I've been stewing over this thing all night."

"My secretary has your address?" Mason inquired.

"Yes, 3902 Washington Street. I've got a little jobbing house there—in automotive parts—piston rings, gaskets and that sort of stuff."

"Own it yourself or working for someone?"

"I own it myself. I'm fed up working for other people. I was a salesman for years. I traveled on rattling trains, ruined my stomach eating poor food, and made a lot of money for the smart boys that stayed at home and owned the business."

He winked his glass eye significantly.

"I got that," he said, "in a train wreck back in 1911. You can see the scar on the side of my head—knocked me out cold. I was in the hospital for two weeks, and it was a month after that before I knew who I was—loss of memory. It lost me my eye and ruined my life."

Mason nodded sympathetically and said, "All right, Brunold; if anything happens, you get in touch with me. If I'm not in the office, you call Della Street, my secretary, and talk with her. She's in my confidence and knows all about the business of the people who call on me."

"Will she keep her mouth shut?" Brunold asked.

Mason laughed. "Torture," he said, "wouldn't get a word out of her."

"How about money?"

"No chance."

"How about flattery? How about someone making love to her? She's a woman, you know, and a mighty attractive one at that."

Mason's shake of his head was accompanied by a frown.

"*You* worry about the things that concern *you*," he said. "*I'll* worry about the things that concern *me*."

Brunold started toward the door through which he had entered.

"You can," Mason said, "get out this other way. This door leads directly to the corridor. . . ."

He broke off as the telephone bell on his private line rang insistently. He scooped the receiver to his ear, and heard Della Street's voice on the other end of the line.

"There's a Miss Bertha McLane here, Chief. She has a younger brother with her—a Harry McLane. They seem to be pretty much excited. She won't tell me the nature of her business. She's been crying, and the brother is surly. They look promising. Will you see them?"

"Okay," he told her; "I'll see them in a minute," and dropped the receiver back into position.

Brunold, halfway through the door, said, "I left my hat in this other office. I'll have to go out that way."

He turned toward the outer office, stiffened suddenly and said, "Hello, Harry; what the devil are you doing here?"

Mason crossed the office in four swift strides, caught Brunold by the shoulder of his coat, jerked him back. "You wait here," he said. "This is a law office, not a club room. I don't want my other clients to see you, and I don't want you to see my other clients."

He pushed his head through the door and said, "Della, bring this man his hat."

When Della Street brought in Brunold's hat, Mason signaled her to close the door.

"Who was it?" he asked Brunold.

"Just young McLane," Brunold said, trying to be casual.

"Know him?"

"Just slightly."

"Know he was coming here?"

"No."

"Know his business here?"

"No."

"Then what made you turn pale?"

"Did I turn pale?"

"Yes."

"I don't know why I did it. Young McLane is nothing to me."

Mason put his hand on Brunold's shoulder. "Well," he said,

"you can go out this way, and . . . Good heavens, man, you're shaking like a leaf!"

"Just nervousness," Brunold said, breaking away and lunging through the door to the outer corridor. "That McLane boy means nothing to me, but the sight of him brings up certain ideas that . . ."

He stepped into the corridor, stopping abruptly in midsentence. The door slammed behind him.

Perry Mason turned to Della Street.

"Get Paul Drake," he said, "of the Drake Detective Bureau, right away. Keep those two people waiting until after I've had a chance to see Drake. Tell Drake to come down to the corridor door and knock. I'll let him in."

She slipped through the door to the outer office, saying to the waiting couple, "Mr. Mason is busy, but he'll see you in a few minutes."

Perry Mason lit a cigarette, started thoughtfully pacing the office. He was still pacing up and down when a tap sounded at the exit door which led to the corridor. Mason threw back the spring lock, opened the door, and nodded to a tall individual with glassy eyes, and a mouth which was twisted into an expression of droll humor.

"Come in, Paul," he said, "and get an earful of this."

The lawyer took from his pocket the glass eye which Brunold had given him, and passed it over to Paul Drake.

The detective examined it curiously.

"Know anything about glass eyes, Paul?"

"Not very much."

"Well, you're going to know a lot in the near future."

"All right, shoot."

"Go to the Baltimore Hotel, engage a room, look through the classified directory and pick someone who's a wholesaler of artificial eyes. Ring him up. Tell him you're a dealer from out of town; that you've got a customer who wants half a dozen bloodshot eyes to match an eye you're sending over by messenger. Give a phony name. Say you come from some outlying city, and that you're just starting in business.

"The wholesaler will have a bunch of eyes in stock. They

won't be as good as the eyes that are made to order by experts. From all I can gather, it's about the same difference as getting a tailor-made suit, or one of the cheaper ready-mades. But the wholesaler can match this eye and then bloodshot the duplicates."

"What do you mean—bloodshot the duplicates?" Drake inquired.

"Putting veins on the outside of them. They do it with red glass. They'll make a rush job of it for you if they think you're going to be a good future customer. Impress that on them, that you're a new dealer from some outlying town."

"How much will the eyes cost?"

"I don't know—ten or twelve dollars apiece, probably."

"You don't want me to go around there and talk with the dealer personally?"

"No. I don't want him to know what you look like. I don't want him to be able to trace you. Register at the hotel under a phony name. Give the dealer the phony name. Keep out of sight as much as possible. Don't tip the bell boys too much or too little. Don't have too much baggage and don't have too little. Be just an ordinary customer of the type that no one will remember if anyone starts checking up on you later on."

Paul Drake's dubious eyes stared steadily at the lawyer.

"Will someone check up on me?" he asked.

"Probably."

"Am I violating any laws, Perry?"

"Nothing that I can't get you out of, Paul."

"Okay. When do I go?"

"Right now."

Drake slipped the eye in his pocket, nodded and turned toward the door.

Perry Mason picked up the telephone and said to Della Street, "All right, Della; I'll see Miss McLane and her brother."

2

BERTHA MCLANE SPOKE IN A LOW, SHARP TONE TO THE YOUNG man who accompanied her. He shook his head, mumbled something in an undertone, and turned to Perry Mason.

Mason indicated chairs.

"You're Miss Bertha McLane?" he asked.

She nodded, turned toward the younger man.

"My brother, Harry."

Mason waited until they were seated, then said, in a kindly voice, "What was it you wanted to see me about?"

She held him with eyes in which there glinted a vigorous determination.

"Who," she asked, "was the man who just left here?"

Perry Mason raised his eyebrows.

"I thought *you* knew him. I heard him speak to you."

"He didn't speak to me. He spoke to Harry."

"Harry can tell you who he is, then."

"Harry won't tell me. He says it's none of my business. I want *you* to tell me."

The lawyer shook his head, and smiled. After a moment he said, in a kindly voice, "What was it *you* wished to see me about?"

"I've got to know who that man was."

The smile left the lawyer's face.

"After all," he said, "this is a law office, you know, not an information bureau."

For a moment there was flashing anger in her eyes. Then she controlled herself.

"After all," she said, "perhaps you're right. If anyone came into *my* office and tried to find out something about who the man was who was just going out, I'd . . . I'd . . ."

"You'd what?" Perry Mason prompted.

She laughed, and said, "Probably lie to him, and tell him I didn't know."

Mason opened a cigarette case and offered her a cigarette.

She hesitated a moment, then took one of the cigarettes, tapped it on her thumb-nail with a practiced hand, leaned forward to the flame of the match which Mason held for her, and inhaled deeply. Mason offered a cigarette to Harry McLane, who shook his head in silent refusal. Mason, himself, lit a cigarette, settled back in the chair and looked from the young man to the young woman, then kept his eyes on Bertha McLane, as though expecting her to do the talking.

She adjusted her skirt, and said, "Harry is in trouble."

Harry McLane shifted uneasily in his chair.

"Tell him about it, Harry," she pleaded.

"You tell him," Harry McLane said, speaking in that mumbling undertone which he had used before.

"Did you," she asked the lawyer, "ever hear of Hartley Basset?"

"Seems to me I've heard the name over the radio. Doesn't he make automobile loans?"

"Yes," she said, with feeling in her voice; "he does. He makes all sorts of loans. The automobile loans he makes, he advertises over the radio. He makes other loans that he doesn't advertise so much, and he isn't above buying a piece of stolen jewelry, or financing an expert smuggler."

The lawyer raised his eyebrows quizzically and started to say something, but puffed on his cigarette instead.

"You can't prove all of that stuff," Harry McLane said, in a surly undertone.

"*You* told me."

"Well, I was just guessing at lots of it."

"No, you weren't, Harry. You know that you were telling the truth. You've worked for him, and you know the kind of business he's running."

"What sort of trouble is Harry in?" Mason inquired.

"He embezzled something over three thousand dollars from Hartley Basset."

The lawyer's eyes shifted to Harry McLane. Harry McLane

met his gaze defiantly for a moment, then dropped his eyes
and said, in a voice so low that it could hardly be heard, "I
was going to pay him back."

"Does Mr. Basset know about it?" Mason inquired.

"He does now."

"When did he find it out?"

"Yesterday."

"Just how did the embezzlement take place?" Mason inquired, turning to the young man. "Was it over a long period
of time? Was it in one sum, or was it in smaller sums, and
what was done with the money?"

Harry McLane looked expectantly toward his sister. She
said, "It was in four separate amounts—almost a thousand dollars each."

"How was it done?"

"It was done by substituting forged notes for original ones."

The lawyer frowned, and said, "I don't see just how that
would be an embezzlement, unless the original notes were
negotiated."

Harry McLane, raising his voice for the first time since he
had entered the room, said, "You don't need to go into all
those details, Sis; just tell him what you want done."

"What *do* you want me to do?" Mason inquired.

"I want you to return the money to Mr. Basset. That is,
I want you to arrange it so *I* can return the money to Mr.
Basset."

"All of it?" Mason asked.

"Eventually, yes. I've only got a little over fifteen hundred
dollars to give him now. I'll give him the balance in installments."

"You're working?" Mason asked.

"Yes."

"Where?"

She flushed and said, "I don't think it's necessary to go into
that, is it?"

"It might be," he told her.

"We can go into it later if we have to. I'm secretary to an
important business man."

"What salary do you make?"

"Is it necessary to go into that?"

"Yes."

"Why?"

"So I can decide how much to charge for my services, for one thing," Mason told her.

"It isn't as much as it should be, considering the work I'm doing. The employees have all had to take substantial reductions."

"How much?" Mason asked.

"Forty dollars a week."

"Anyone dependent on you?"

"My mother."

"Living with you?"

"No, in Denver."

"How much do you send her?"

"Seventy dollars a month."

"You're her sole support?"

"Yes."

"How about Harry?"

"He hasn't been able to send anything."

"He's been working for Hartley Basset?"

"Yes."

"How much salary," Mason inquired, "did Harry get?"

Harry McLane said, "I couldn't help Mother out on what I was getting."

"How much was it?"

"A hundred dollars a month."

"It takes more for a man to live than a woman," Bertha McLane said.

"How long did you work for Basset?"

"Six months."

Mason studied the young man, then said curtly, "And, in that time, you made something over seven hundred and fifty dollars a month, did you not?"

Sheer surprise caused Harry McLane's eyes to widen.

"Seven hundred and fifty dollars a month!" he exclaimed. "I should say not. Old Basset wouldn't give anyone a decent salary. He paid me a hundred dollars a month, and hated like hell to part with it."

"During that time," Mason said, "you embezzled something like four thousand dollars. Added to your salary, that makes your monthly income around seven hundred and fifty dollars a month."

Harry McLane's lips quivered at the corners. He said, "You can't figure it that way," and lapsed into silence.

"Any of that money go to your mother?" Mason asked.

It was Bertha McLane who answered the question.

"No," she said, "we don't know where it went."

Mason turned again to the boy.

"Where did it go, Harry?"

"It's gone."

"Where?"

"I tell you it's gone."

"I want to know where it went."

"Why do you want to know that?"

"Because I've got to know it if I'm going to help you."

"A fat lot of help you're being."

Mason pounded his fist on the desk with slow deliberation, beating time to his words with the pounding of the fist.

"If you think," he said, "that I'm going to try to help you without knowing the facts of the case, you're crazy. Now, are you going to tell me the facts, or are you going to find some other lawyer?"

"He gave the money to someone," Bertha McLane said.

"A woman?" Mason inquired.

"No," Harry said, with a flash of something like pride. "I don't have to pay women money. They're willing to give me money."

"Whom did you give it to?"

"I gave it to someone to invest."

"Who?"

"That's something I'm not going to tell."

"You've got to tell."

"I'm not going to tell. I'm not going to rat on anyone. That's one of the things you can't make me do. Sis has been trying to make me squeal. I won't squeal. I'll go to jail and stay there until I die before I'll turn rat."

Bertha McLane turned toward him.

"Harry," she said, in a pleading voice, "was it that man who was just here in the office—the man who spoke to you there in the doorway?"

"No," Harry said defiantly; "I just met that bird once."

"Where did you meet him?"

"None of your business."

"What's his name?"

"Leave him out of it."

She turned to Perry Mason, and said, "He had some accomplice, someone who was bleeding him for the money, someone who helped him to rig things up so that he could get the money without being caught."

"*How* did he get the money?" Mason asked.

"He had charge of the note file. Basset charges exorbitant rates of interest. People don't borrow money from him except as a last resort. He gets whatever security he can, and all the interest the law will allow. Sometimes people find that they can raise money from other sources. When they do, they rush in to pay off the notes in order to stop the excessive interest.

"That's what happened in these cases. People came in to pay off the notes. They paid the money to Harry. Harry took the money and gave them back their notes. Then he forged notes with their signatures, and put the forged notes back in the note file. Whenever Mr. Basset checked up on the note file, it seemed to be all right, because these forged notes were in there. And Harry kept the interest paid on the forged notes."

"How was he detected?" Mason asked.

"One of the notes came due. Harry couldn't get the money to meet the note immediately. He thought he'd have a few days. He stalled along, but Mr. Basset happened to see the man who'd given the note at a golf club. He dunned him for the money, and the man told him he'd paid off the note four months ago. He had the original note, marked 'Canceled,' to prove his claim. So Basset made a complete investigation."

"What makes you think Harry had an accomplice?"

"He's admitted that much to me. It was the accomplice that got the money. I think he was taking it to gamble with."

"What sort of gambling?"

"All sorts—poker, roulette, horse racing, and lottery, principally horse racing and lottery."

"If the old fool had just sat tight, I'd have got him his money back—all of it," Harry McLane said.

Perry Mason turned to Bertha McLane, studied her with level, appraising eyes.

"The fifteen hundred dollars," he said, "represents your savings?"

"It's money that I have in a savings bank—yes."

"Money you've saved out of your salary?"

"Yes."

"You've got to keep on sending your mother seventy dollars a month?"

"Yes."

"You want to pay this amount off so Harry won't have to go to jail?"

"Yes; it would kill Mother."

"And then you intend to make payments out of your salary?"

"Yes."

"Harry is out of a job," Mason said; "you'll have him on your hands to support."

"Don't worry about me," Harry McLane said. "I'll get by all right. I'll get a job and pay Sis back every cent of it. She won't have to pay anything out of her salary. I'll get it all back to her inside of thirty days."

"Just how," asked Perry Mason, "did you intend to get it back?"

"I'm going to get it back. I'll make some investments. I can't run into bad luck all the time."

"In other words," Mason said, "you intend to keep on gambling."

"I didn't say so."

"What are the investments you had in mind?"

"I don't have to tell you what my investments are going to be. You just go ahead and get this thing fixed up with Basset. I'll handle my affairs with Sis."

Mason's tone was final.

"I'll give you my advice right now," he said. "Don't pay Basset one cent."

"But I've got to; the money was taken from him."

"Don't pay him a single thin dime."

"He's given me until tomorrow night to get the money for him, and then he's going to put the thing in the hands of the district attorney," Harry McLane said, as though the lawyer had failed to comprehend the situation.

"Jail," Mason said, "is the proper place for you, young man!"

Bertha McLane's eyes widened.

"I've been in the law business a long time," Mason told them. "I've seen them come and I've seen them go. I've seen men of this type before. Their first crime is usually a small crime. Someone covers it up, with a great deal of sacrifice. Now, I'm willing to bet you ten to one that this isn't the first time you've had to make good for Harry—is it?"

Harry McLane blurted, "That's got nothing to do with it. Who the hell do you think you are, anyway?"

Perry Mason did not take his eyes from Bertha McLane's face.

"*Is* it the first time?" he asked.

"I've had to cover a check or two," she said slowly.

"Exactly!" he told her. "Your brother is sliding. You're doing your best to keep him from it. He knows that he's got you back of him all the time. He started out giving a bum check. You made it good. He was sorry and promised you he'd never do it again. He talked big. He was going out and get a job. He was going to do this and he was going to do that. Talk is cheap. But, it's the only coin he's got with which to pay anyone anything. He hypnotizes himself into believing that he's going to do what he says he's going to do. But he hasn't got guts enough to go out and do it. He doesn't intend to get a job. He intends to get some more money from you in order to play a 'sure thing.' Then he thinks he'll make a 'big killing' and come in with his pockets lined with money.

"He's one of those fellows who want to be 'big shots.' He hasn't got guts enough to go out and do it by hard work. Therefore, he does it with talk and by trying to take short cuts. When things go wrong, he feels sorry for himself and wants someone to listen to his tale of woe. When he has a little spurt of good fortune, he patronizes all of his friends and starts to strut. Then the next time he gets a body blow, he caves in and crawls all over the place, trying to put his head in your lap and sob out his troubles, while you run your fingers through his hair, tell him you'll protect him and that it will be all right.

"The thing this young man needs is to be forced to live his own life. He's been dependent on women too long. He's a younger brother. You've fought his battles. I presume his father's dead and you put him through school. Right?"

"I put him through business college. I made a stenographer and bookkeeper of him. That was the best I could do. Sometimes I blame myself. I think I should have tried a little harder to give him a better education. But, after Father's death, I had Mother to support, and . . ."

Harry McLane got to his feet.

"Come on, Sis," he said. "It's easy enough for a guy who collects big fees to sit in a swivel chair and read lectures to a bird who's had all the breaks against him. We don't have to stick around and listen to it."

"On the contrary," Perry Mason told him, "you do."

He got to his feet and pointed to the chair.

"Get back there and sit down," he said.

Harry McLane stared at him with sullen defiance. Mason took a quick step toward him and McLane dropped into the chair.

Mason turned back to Bertha McLane.

"You wanted to get legal advice," he said. "I'm giving it to you. You can't cover up this embezzlement, with the understanding that Basset isn't going to prosecute your brother, unless you compound a felony. Moreover, from the income that you have at your command, you can't hope to keep up regular monthly payments to Basset, support your mother, pay your own living expenses, and, at the same time, pay out the money that your brother will be nicking you for every month in order to keep up with his gambling.

"I'll try to get this young man probation. But, in order to get probation, he'll have to cut out all of his gambling associations. He'll have to tell the court who got this money and what was done with it. He'll have to quit acting the part of a spoiled kid with an indulgent sister, and learn to stand on his own two feet, and it *may* make a man of him."

"But you don't understand," Bertha McLane said, in a voice that seemed perilously close to the breaking point. "I've got to pay back the money anyway. It was embezzled by my brother. I wouldn't care whether he went to jail or whether he didn't. I'd turn over the money to Mr. Basset just as fast as I could get it."

"How old are you?" Mason inquired.

"Twenty-seven."

"How old's the boy?"

"Twenty-two."

"Why should you be obligated to pay off his embezzlement?"

"Because he's my brother. And then, there's my mother to be considered. Can't you understand she's not at all well. She isn't young. Harry is the apple of her eye."

"Her favorite?" Mason asked.

"Well," she said slowly, "of course, he's the man of the family. Ever since Father died, he's been the man—that is, he's been . . ."

"I know," Perry Mason said. "He's been the one you've slaved for and given all the breaks. Can't you explain the facts to your mother?"

"Good Lord, no! It would kill her. She thinks Harry is a big business man; that he's been Mr. Basset's right-hand man; that Mr. Basset is one of the biggest financiers in the city."

Perry Mason drummed on his desk.

"And you're going to pay the money whether Basset prosecutes or not?"

"Yes."

Mason stared down at Harry McLane.

"Young man," he said, "you say you've never got the breaks. When you go to bed tonight, get down on your knees and thank God that you've got an invalid mother. Because I'm going out against my better judgment and try and compound a felony. But I'm going to keep in touch with you, and I'm either going to put some manhood in you, or I'm going to bust you wide open."

He picked up the telephone on his desk, and said to Della Street, "Get me Hartley Basset. He's in the loan business."

He held the receiver in his hand, turned to Bertha McLane, and said, "You're going to have trouble with Hartley Basset. He's going to want you to give him everything you've got, including your soul. He's the type who will drive a hard bargain."

Harry McLane said, "Don't worry about Hartley Basset. You make him the best kind of a proposition we can make, and Basset is going to accept it."

"Where do you get that noise," Mason said scornfully. "The best proposition *we* can make."

"Well, it's Sis and I together," McLane said. "I'm going to pay her off."

Mason nodded his head, and said, "You may not think so now, but you are. I'm going to see that you do. But what makes you so confident Basset will accept your proposition?"

"He's got to. There's going to be pressure brought to bear on him."

"By whom?"

"By someone that's in his house, who's friendly to me."

"You are the type who makes fair-weather friends," Mason told him. "A man who hasn't any more character than you have doesn't make friends who stick by him."

"That's what you think," McLane said defiantly. "You're going to be fooled. You'll find that there's someone who can make Basset do anything, who's going to be sticking up for me. You just make your proposition and don't pay any attention to what Basset says at the time. He'll probably tell you no, but, within an hour, he'll ring you up on the telephone and tell you he's reconsidered, and that he's willing to accept it."

Perry Mason, staring down at the young man, said in slow, measured words, "Have you been playing around with Mrs. Basset?"

Young McLane flushed and started to answer. The telephone made sounds, and Mason put the receiver to his ear.

"Hello," he said, "Basset? . . . Is this Mr. Hartley Basset? Well, this is Perry Mason, the lawyer. I've got a matter I want to take up with you. Can you come to my office? . . . All right, I'll come to yours. Sometime this evening? . . . Yes, I can make it this evening all right. I'd prefer to make it this afternoon. . . . Well, this evening will be all right. You have your office at your house, you say? I'll be there at eight-thirty. . . . Oh, you know what it's about, then. . . . Very well, eight-thirty."

Perry Mason dropped the receiver back into position.

"How did Basset know that you were going to come here?" he asked.

Harry McLane, his manner filled with assurance, said, "He knew it because I told him."

"You told him?" Bertha McLane asked.

"Yes," Harry said. "He was doing a lot of talking about sending me to jail and all that stuff, and I thought it would be a good plan to throw a scare into him. I told him that Perry Mason was going to be my lawyer, and he'd better watch his own step, or Perry Mason might see to it that he was the one who went to jail."

Mason stared at Harry McLane in silent dislike.

Bertha McLane crossed to him, put her hand on his arm.

"Thank you," she said, "ever so much. And remember that I'll do the very most that I can for Mr. Basset. I'll pay him off just as quickly as possible—the whole amount and interest. I'll execute a note for it. He can charge interest at the rate of one percent a month. That's what he charges on his notes, you know."

Mason took a deep breath, and said slowly, "As far as Hartley Basset is concerned, I'll talk to him." He took from his desk a blank piece of white bond paper, scribbled a number on it in pencil, handed it to Bertha McLane and said, "This is the telephone number of my apartment. You can reach me there whenever I'm not at the office if anything important should develop. I think your brother's going to talk. When he does, I want to hear what he says."

"You mean about his accomplice?"

"Yes," Mason said.

Harry McLane, his manner now showing brazen self-assurance, contented himself with one comment.

"Nerts," he said.

Bertha McLane pretended not to hear him.

"Your fees," she asked, "how much will they be?"

Mason grinned at her and said, "Forget it. The man who just went out of the office paid me enough for his case and yours, too."

3

A SEPARATE DOOR, MARKED: "BASSET AUTO FINANCE COMPANY. Walk In" was immediately to the right of the door on which a brass placard bore the legend:

HARTLEY BASSET—RESIDENCE
Private
No Peddlers or Solicitors

Perry Mason opened the door which led to the office, and walked in. The outer office was deserted. A door marked

"PRIVATE" was at the further end. Above an electric push-button appeared the words, "RING AND BE SEATED."

Perry Mason rang.

Almost immediately the door opened. A deep-chested man, with a close-cropped gray mustache and a thick shock of hair which had grizzled at the temples, stared at him with light-gray eyes, from the centers of which pin-pointed black pupils held a hypnotic fascination.

Moving with quick virility, he shot out his left wrist so that he could stare at the wrist watch.

"On time," he said, "to the minute."

Perry Mason bowed, said nothing, and followed Hartley Basset into a rather plainly appointed office.

"Not here," Basset said; "this is where I collect money. I don't want it to look too prosperous. Come into the office from which I make my big loans. I like it better in there."

He opened a door and indicated an office sumptuously furnished. From a room beyond came the sound of a clacking typewriter.

"Work nights?" Perry Mason asked.

"I'm usually open for a couple of hours during the evening. That's to accommodate people who have jobs. A man who isn't working and wants to borrow on an automobile isn't as good a risk as the man who has a job and needs money."

He indicated a chair. Mason dropped into it.

"You want to see me about Harry McLane?" Basset asked.

At the lawyer's nod, Basset pressed a button. The type-writing in the adjoining office ceased. A chair made a noise as it scraped back. Then a door opened. A narrow-shouldered man, about forty-five years of age, with grayish eyes, peered owlishly from behind horn-rimmed spectacles.

"Arthur," Basset said, "what are the exact figures on the McLane embezzlement?"

"Three thousand, nine hundred and forty-two dollars and sixty-three cents," the man in the doorway said, his voice husky and without expression.

"That includes interest?" asked Basset, "at the rate of one per cent a month?"

"Interest at the rate of one per cent a month," the man affirmed, "from the date the money was embezzled."

Basset said, "That's all."

The man in the doorway stepped back and closed the door. A few seconds later, the clack of the typewriter sounded with mechanical regularity. Hartley Basset smiled at Perry Mason, and said, "He's got until tomorrow afternoon."

Mason extracted a cigarette from his cigarette case. Basset pulled a cigar from his waistcoat pocket. Both men lit up at virtually the same time. Mason extinguished his match by blowing smoke on it, and said, "There's no reason why you and I should misunderstand each other."

"None whatever," Basset agreed.

"I don't know the facts of the case," Mason went on, "but I'm acting on the assumption that McLane embezzled the money."

"He's confessed to it."

"Well, let's not argue that point. Let's assume that he *did* embezzle it."

"Saving the point so you can defend him in court?" Basset asked, his eyes growing hard.

"I'm simply not making any admissions," Mason said. "If my clients want to make admissions they can do so. I never make admissions."

"Go ahead," Basset remarked.

"You want your money."

"Naturally."

"McLane hasn't got it."

"He had an accomplice."

"Do you know who the accomplice was?"

"No. I wish I did."

"Why?"

"Because the accomplice has the money."

"What makes you think so?"

"I'm virtually certain of it."

"Why doesn't the accomplice pay it back then?"

"I don't know all of the reasons. One of them is that the accomplice is a gambler. He has to have a roll in order to gamble. You dig into Harry McLane's mental processes deeply enough, and you'll find that he's figuring on staging a big comeback. He's got sense enough to know that if he and his accomplice pay back all the money Harry embezzled, they won't have any operating capital. A gambler needs something to gamble with.

"Not that I blame them particularly," Basset said, "if they can get away with it. But they can't get away with it. Not with *my* money. They're either going to kick through, or go to jail."

"I presume you realize," Mason said, "that you're compounding a felony."

"I'm doing nothing of the sort. I'm getting my money back."

"You're offering embezzlers immunity from prosecution if they make good the money embezzled."

"Let's not be overly technical about it," Basset remarked. "You know what you want. I know what I want. I'm talking plainly to you. I might not talk as plainly elsewhere. I want my money."

"And you think McLane has it?"

"No, I think his accomplice has it."

"But don't you think if McLane could get it from his accomplice, he'd have done so already?"

"No," Basset said. "They stole money to gamble with. They lost some of it. They want to keep on gambling. McLane's sister will put up money to keep McLane from going to jail. That will leave the pair money to gamble with."

"Well?" Mason asked.

"The girl hasn't *all* of the money," Basset said. "She's got a little over fifteen hundred dollars. McLane's accomplice has about two thousand left. I'll get the girl's money and then I'll find out who the accomplice is and get what money he's got."

"Suppose," Mason asked, "it doesn't work that way?"

"It will."

Mason said slowly, "I can get you fifteen hundred dollars in cash and monthly payments of thirty dollars. I'm representing the sister."

"Her money?" Basset asked.

"Yes."

"All of it?"

"Yes."

"The boy hasn't kicked through with any of it?"

"No."

"I'll take the fifteen hundred cash and a hundred a month from the girl," Basset said.

Mason flushed, sucked in a quick breath, controlled himself, puffed on the cigarette, and said tonelessly, "She can't do it. She's supporting an invalid mother. She can't live on what would be left of her salary."

"I'm not interested," Basset said, "in getting my money back in small installments. Monthly payments of one hundred dollars will get the principal reduced reasonably so that Harry McLane may get a job in the meantime. He can pass the loss on to his new employer."

"What do you mean," Mason inquired, "by passing the loss on to his new employer?"

"He can work out some scheme of embezzling from his new employer to pay me off my losses."

"You mean you'd force him to theft?"

"Certainly not. I'm simply suggesting that he pass on the burden. He embezzled from me. I held the sack for a while. Let someone else hold it for a while now."

Mason laughed. "You might find yourself an accessory before the fact in that new embezzlement, Basset."

Basset stared coldly at him and said, "What do I care. I want my money. I don't care how I get it. There's no legal evidence against me. The moral aspect of the case leaves me completely indifferent."

"I gathered it did," Mason told him.

"That's fine. It eliminates misunderstandings. I'm not going to talk with you about the morals of *your* profession and you're not going to talk with me about the morals of mine. I want my money. You're here to see that I get it. The sister doesn't want the boy to go to jail. I've given you my terms. That's all there is to it."

"Those terms," Mason told him, "won't be met."

Basset shrugged his shoulders and said, "He's got until tomorrow."

Knuckles sounded in a gentle knock on the panels of the door, which almost immediately opened. A woman, between thirty-five and forty, glanced at Perry Mason with a quick half smile, and turned solicitously to Hartley Basset. "May I sit in on this, Hartley?" she asked.

Hartley Basset remained seated. He regarded her through the smoke which twisted upward from the cigar. His face had no flicker of expression.

"My wife," he said to the lawyer.

Mason got to his feet, surveyed the slender figure appreciatively, and said, "I am very pleased, Mrs. Basset."

She kept her eyes fastened apprehensively upon her husband.

"Please, Hartley, I'd like to have something to say about this."

"Why?"

"Because I'm interested."

"Interested in what?"

"Interested in what you're going to do."

"Do you mean," he asked, "that you're interested in Harry McLane?"

"No. I'm interested for another reason."

"What's the other reason?"

"I don't want you to be too hard if the money is coming from his sister."

"I think," Basset said, "I'm the best judge of that."

"May I sit in on your conference?"

The eyes were cold and hard. The voice was utterly without emotion, as Basset said, "No."

There was a moment of silence. Basset did nothing to soften the curtness of his refusal. Mrs. Basset hesitated a moment, then turned and walked across the office. She didn't leave through the door by which she had entered, but went, instead, into the adjoining office, and a moment later, the sound of a closing door announced that she had gone through it to the reception room.

Hartley Basset said, "No need for you to sit down again, Mason; we understand each other perfectly. Good night."

Perry Mason strode to the door, jerked it open, called back over his shoulder, "Good night, and goodby."

He strode across the outer office, slammed the door of the reception room behind him, and crossed the porch in three swift strides. He crossed to the left side of his coupé, jerked open the door and was just sliding in behind the wheel when he realized someone was huddled at the opposite end of the seat.

He stiffened to quick vigilance, and a woman's voice said, "Just close the door, please, and drive around the corner."

It was the voice of Mrs. Basset.

Mason hesitated a moment. His face showed irritation, then curiosity. He slid behind the wheel, drove around the block, stopped, and switched off lights and motor. Mrs. Basset leaned forward, put her hand on his sleeve, and said, "Please do what he asks."

"What he asks," he said, "is humanly impossible."

"No, it isn't impossible," she said. "I know him too well for that. He'll get blood out of a turnip. He'll get the last drop of blood, but he'll never ask for something that's impossible."

"The girl's supporting an invalid mother."

"But surely," Mrs. Basset said, "there's charitable aid for such people. After all, the girl doesn't *have* to do it. People don't starve to death in civilized communities, you know. If the girl should die, you know, the mother would be taken care of some way."

Mason said, savagely, "And you think the girl should try to live on sixty dollars a month, and cut off her mother without a cent; all in order to pay back your husband money that's been embezzled from him by a no account kid?"

"No," she said. "Not to get him back his money. To keep him from doing what he'll do if he *doesn't* get his money back."

Mason said slowly, "And you sneaked out here to tell me that?"

"No," she told him; "to ask you something. I just mentioned about that embezzlement incidentally."

"If you want to consult me," he told her, "come to my office."

"I *can't* come to your office. I never get away. I'm spied on all the time."

"Don't be foolish," Mason told her. "Who'd want to spy on you?"

"My husband, of course."

"Do you mean to say you couldn't come to a lawyer's office if you wanted to?"

"Certainly I couldn't."

"Who would stop you?"

"He would."

"How would he do it?"

"I don't know how. He'd do it. He's utterly ruthless. He'd kill me if I crossed him."

Mason frowned thoughtfully and said, "What was it you wanted to ask me about?"

"Bigamy."

"What about it?"

"I'm married to Hartley Basset."

"So I understand."

"I want to run away and leave him."

"Go ahead."

"I have another man who wants to support me."

"Swell."

"I'd have to marry him."

"Then you could get a divorce from Basset."

"But I'd have to marry him at once."

"You mean you'd go through a marriage ceremony without getting a divorce from Basset?"

"Yes."

"Then this man doesn't know you're married to Basset?"

"Yes," she said slowly; "he does."

"He wants to become a party to a bigamous marriage?"

"We want to fix it so it isn't bigamy."

"You could," Perry Mason said, "get a quick divorce by going to certain places."

"Would he have to know anything about it?"

"Yes."

"Then I couldn't get it."

"Then you couldn't get married."

"I could get married, couldn't I? It would be only a question of whether the marriage was legal or illegal."

"You'd have to perjure yourself in order to get a license."

"Well, suppose I perjured myself—what then?"

The lawyer, turning to study her profile, said, "You mentioned something about being followed. I presume you noticed the automobile parked close to the curb behind us?"

"Good God, no!" she said.

She whirled around so that she could look through the rear window, and gave a stifled half scream.

"My God, it's James!"

"Who is James?"

"My husband's chauffeur."

"That your husband's car?"

"Yes, one of them."

"You think the chauffeur followed you?"

"I know it. I thought I had slipped away from him, but I didn't."

"What do you want to do now; get out?"

"No. Drive around the block and let me out at the house."

"The man in the car behind," Mason said, "knows that you've seen him."

"I can't help that. Please do as I say. Please, at once!"

Mason drove the car around the block. The car which had been parked behind him switched on headlights and followed doggedly. Mason slid the car to the curb in front of Basset's residence, leaned across the woman and opened the door.

"If you want to consult me," he said, "I'll come in."

"No, no!" she half screamed.

A figure moved from the shadows, stepped up close to

the car, and Hartley Basset said, "Did you, by any chance, have a rendezvous with my wife?"

Mason opened the door on his side of the car, got out, crossed around the rear of the car, and stood toe to toe with Hartley Basset. "No," he said, "I didn't."

"Then," Basset said, "my wife must have arranged a meeting. Was she trying to consult you about something?" Mason braced himself, feet wide apart.

"The reason I got out of the car," he said, "and walked over here, was to tell you to mind your own damned business."

The other car which had followed Mason had parked close to the curb. A tall, thin man who walked with a quick, cat-like step, opened the car door, started toward Mason, then, as he heard the tone of Mason's voice, turned back to the car, took something from a side pocket in the door and walked rapidly toward the lawyer, approaching him from the rear. The headlights gleamed on a wrench which he held in his right hand.

The lawyer swung around so that he faced both men. Mrs. Basset ran up the steps to the house, slammed the door shut behind her.

"Do you birds," Mason asked ominously, "want to start something?"

Basset looked over at the tall man with the wrench.

"That's all, James," he said.

Mason stared at them steadily, then said slowly, "You're damn' right that's all."

He turned to his own car, slid behind the wheel, and kicked in the clutch. The pair behind him stood watching him, silhouetted against the headlights of the parked car.

The lawyer swung his car into a skidding turn and straightened into swift speed as he hit the main boulevard.

He braked the car to a stop when he came to a drug store, walked to the telephone booth, dialed a number, and, when he heard Bertha McLane's anxious voice, said, "It's all off."

"Wouldn't he accept it?"

"No."

"What did he want?"

"Something that was impossible."

"What was it?"

"It was impossible."

"But, at least you must tell me what it was."

"He wanted you to pay one hundred dollars a month."

"But I couldn't!"

"That's what I told him. I told him you had a mother to support. He feels that your mother can go on public charity."

"Oh, but I couldn't do that!"

"That's what I told him. Now listen. You make Harry tell you what he's done with the money, and who his accomplice is."

"But Harry won't do it."

"Then let him go to jail."

"Where are you now?"

"At a drug store."

"Near Basset's place?"

"Yes."

"Go back and tell Mr. Basset I'll arrange to get the money some way. I can meet the payments for one or two months at least. By that time, Harry will be working. I have some things I can sell."

"I'll tell Basset nothing of the sort."

"But I want to accept his offer before Harry goes to jail."

"You have until tomorrow afternoon to get some other attorney to act for you."

"You mean you won't represent me?"

"No," Mason said; "not to accept any such offer as that. The only way I'll represent you is for you to let me take your kid brother apart and see what makes him tick. After he comes clean, I'll do the best for you that I can. Otherwise, you get some other lawyer. Don't argue with me over the telephone. Think it over. Give me your answer later."

He banged up the receiver.

4

PERRY MASON, SPRAWLED IN AN EASY CHAIR, READING A BOOK on the latest discoveries in psychology, barely noticed the clock strike midnight.

The telephone on the stand at his elbow made noise. Mason picked up the receiver and said, "Hello, Mason speaking." He heard a woman's voice, harsh with emotion, spilling words into his ear before he had placed her identity.

". . . Come out at once. I'm leaving my husband. He's been guilty of a brutal attack. There's going to be trouble. My son is going to kill him. . . ."

"Who is this talking?" Mason interrupted.

"Sylvia Basset—Hartley Basset's wife."

"What do you want me to do?"

"Come out here just as soon as you can get here."

"It'll keep," the lawyer said, "until morning."

"No; it won't. You don't understand. A woman out here has been seriously injured."

"What's the matter with her?"

"She's been struck over the head."

"Who struck her?"

"My husband."

"Where's your husband?"

"He jumped in a car and ran away. As soon as he comes back, my son, Dick, is going to kill him. There isn't a thing that I can do to stop it. I want you to come out and take charge of the case. If my husband comes back before you get here, Dick will kill him. I want you to explain to Dick that you can protect my interests; that he doesn't need to take the law in his own hands; that . . ."

"Where are you now?"

"At my home."

34

"Can you bring your son to me?"

"No, he won't leave. He's furious. I can't do anything with him."

"Have you threatened to call in the police?"

"No."

"Why?"

"Because they'd arrest him, and I don't want that, and there are other things that would make it very embarrassing for me. Won't you please come out? I can't explain over the phone, but it's life and death. It's . . ."

"I'll come out," Perry Mason interrupted. "You keep Dick under control until I get there."

He dropped the receiver into place, flung off his smoking jacket and slippers, struggled into coat and shoes, and one minute and thirty seconds later was pressing the throttle of his coupé down against the floor-boards as he charged through the night streets.

Mrs. Basset met him at the door of the house—the one that had been marked as the entrance to the finance company.

"Come in here," she said, "and please talk with Dick as soon as you can."

Perry Mason entered the outer office. A slender youth of twenty-one or twenty-two jerked open the door from the inner office and said, "Look here, Mom, I'm not going to wait . . ." He broke off as he saw Perry Mason. His hands, which had been extended in front of him, dropped to his sides.

"Dick," she said, "I want you to meet Perry Mason, the lawyer. This is Dick Basset, my son."

The young man stared at Perry Mason with wide, deep, brown eyes. His face was dead-white. The lips of a sensitive, well-formed mouth were clamped into a firm line. Mason extended his hand easily.

"Basset," he said, "I'm glad to know you."

Basset hesitated a moment, regarded Mason's outstretched hand, shifted something from his right hand to his left, and stepped forward.

A small object dropped to the floor. He grabbed Mason's hand, shook it, and said, "Are you representing Mother?"

Mason nodded.

"She's been through hell," the boy said. "I've kept out of it long enough. Tonight I . . ."

He stopped as he saw Perry Mason's eyes come to rest on the thing which had dropped to the carpet.

"Cartridge?" Mason asked.

The boy stooped to recover it, but Mason was first. He picked up a .38 cartridge and stared at it speculatively as he held it in his outstretched hand.

"Why the munitions?" he asked.

"That's my business," Basset said.

Mason reached out, grabbed the boy's left hand, pushed the fingers open before young Basset could define his intentions, disclosed several more .38 caliber shells. One cartridge was empty.

"Where's the gun?" he asked.

"Don't try any of that stuff!" Basset flared. "You can't . . ."

Perry Mason grabbed the young man's shoulder, jerked him forward, spun him around, and, at the same time, slipped an exploring right hand beneath the back of the coat.

Dick Basset tried to struggle, braced himself, and jerked free, but not before Perry Mason had pulled the .38 caliber revolver from the right hip pocket.

Mason broke the gun open. The cylinder was unloaded. He smelled of the muzzle.

"Smells as though it had been fired," he said.

Dick Basset stared at him in white-faced silence. Mrs. Basset jumped forward, wrapped her hands around the gun.

"Oh, *please*," she said to Perry Mason. "I wondered where that was. Please give it to me."

Mason kept his hold on the gun.

"What's the idea?" he asked.

"I want it."

"Whose is it?"

"I don't know."

Mason looked at young Basset and said, "Where did you get it?"

Basset remained silent.

Mason shook his head at Mrs. Basset and gently disengaged her hands.

"I think," he said, "it will be safer with me for a while. Now, what's happened?"

She released her hold on the gun reluctantly, and said to the boy, "You show him, Dick."

Dick Basset pulled aside a Japanese screen, disclosing a corner of the room which had been concealed from the lawyer's gaze.

A broad-hipped woman with faded red hair was bending over someone who lay on a dilapidated couch. She didn't look up as the screen was moved, but said over her shoulder, "I think she's going to be all right in a few minutes. Is this the doctor?"

The lawyer walked to one side so that he could look past the red-headed woman, to see the figure which lay on the couch.

She was a brunette in the middle twenties, attired in a dark suit. The blouse had been opened at the neck to disclose the white curve of a throat and breast. Wet towels lay on the couch near her head. A bottle of smelling-salts and a small bottle of brandy were nestled in among the wet towels. The red-headed woman was chafing the girl's wrists.

"Who is she?" asked Perry Mason.

Mrs. Basset said slowly, "My daughter-in-law—Dick's wife. But no one knows it yet. She's going under her maiden name."

Dick Basset swung around as though about to say something, but remained silent.

Perry Mason indicated a bruise on the side of the young woman's head.

"What happened?"

"My husband struck her."

"Why?"

"I don't know why."

"What with?"

"I don't know. He struck her and then ran out of the house."

"Where did he go?"

"His car was in front. He jumped in it and drove away, going like mad."

"Was the chauffeur with him?"

"No, he was alone in the car."

"Did you see him?"

"Yes."

"Where were you?"

"I saw him from a window in the upper story."

"You know it was his car?"

"Yes. It was his Packard."

"Did he have any bags with him?"

"No, no bags."

The young woman on the couch stirred and moaned.

"She's coming to," the red-headed woman said.

Perry Mason leaned forward. Mrs. Basset stepped to the head of the couch, smoothed back the girl's wet hair, stroked her fingers over the closed eyes, and said, "Hazel, dear, can you hear me?"

The lids fluttered upward, disclosing dark eyes that stared dazedly. The girl retched, moaned and turned to her side.

"She's going to be sick, and then she'll be all right," the older woman said, nodding her head at Sylvia Basset, and turning to stare curiously at Perry Mason.

Perry Mason faced Mrs. Basset.

"Do you want me to take charge of this thing?" he asked.

"In what way?"

"Do you want me to handle it the way I think best?"

"Yes."

Perry Mason stepped to the telephone which was on the battered, cigarette-burnt desk, and said, "Give me police headquarters. . . . Hello, headquarters? This is Richard Basset at 9682 Franklin Street. There's been some trouble out here. I think my father's been drinking, but he's clubbed a woman quite badly. . . . Yes, it's my father. We want him arrested, of course. He's crazy. We can't tell what he'll do next. Please send officers at once. . . . Yes, one of the radio cars is all right, only get here at once, because he may kill someone."

Perry Mason dropped the receiver on its hook, stared at Mrs. Basset.

"You," he said, "keep out of it."

He turned to the boy.

"You go ahead and take the initiative in this thing. I gather that you side with your mother, and against your father?"

Mrs. Basset said, "Of course, it will come out during the investigation that Hartley isn't Dick's father."

"Who was?"

"He's my son by a—a previous marriage."

"How long have you been married to Hartley Basset?"

"Five years."

Dick Basset said bitterly, "Five years of torture."

The woman on the couch stirred and moaned again. She said something that was unintelligible, then coughed and struggled to a sitting position.

"Where am I?" she asked.

"It's all right, Hazel," Mrs. Basset said. "Everything's going to be all right. There's nothing to worry about. We've got a lawyer here, and the police are coming."

The young woman closed her eyes, sighed, and said, "Oh, let me think—let me think."

Mrs. Basset moved close to Perry Mason.

"Please," she said in an undertone, "let me have the gun. I don't want you to have it."

"Why?"

"Because I think we should hide it."

"You're not supposed to have a gun," Mason told her.

"It isn't mine."

"Suppose the police find it?"

"They won't find it if you'll only give it to me. *Please.*"

Perry Mason pulled the gun from his hip pocket and handed it to her. She dropped it down the front of her dress and held it there with her hand.

"You can't leave it there," Mason said. "If you're going to hide it, go ahead and hide it."

"Wait," she told him. "You don't understand. I'll take care of it. . . ."

Dick Basset, bending tenderly over the young woman on the couch, exclaimed, "Good God!"

The girl opened her eyes. Dick kissed her, and she let one of her arms slide around his neck. She talked with him in a low voice. A moment later Dick Basset gently disengaged her arm, and turned to face them.

"It wasn't Hartley who hit her," he said.

"It must have been," Mrs. Basset insisted. "She must be delirious. I came as far as the outer office with her. I knew Hartley was alone."

Dick Basset said, excitedly, "It wasn't Hartley. Hazel didn't even talk with him. She knocked at that door to Dad's office. There was no answer. She opened the door and the office was empty. She crossed the office and knocked at the door of the inner office. Dad opened the door. Someone was with him. She couldn't see who it was. The man had his back to her. Dad told her he was busy, to go back and sit down.

"She waited almost ten minutes. Then that door opened. A man reached through and turned out the lights. He started to run through the office, saw her, and turned. Light from the inner office struck his face. She saw the black mask and the eyes through the black mask. One of the eye sockets was empty. She screamed. He struck at her. She tore off the mask. It was a one-eyed man she'd never seen before in her life. He cursed her and clubbed her with a blackjack. She lost consciousness."

"Only had one eye?" Sylvia Basset cried. "Dick, there's some mistake!" Her voice rose as though with hysteria.

"Only one eye," Dick Basset repeated. "Isn't that right, Hazel?"

The young woman nodded slowly.

"What happened to the mask?" Mason asked.

"She tore it off. It was a paper mask—black paper."

Mason, down on his hands and knees, pulled a sheet of carbon paper from the floor. Eye holes had been cut in it, one corner was torn off. The paper was ripped down the center.

"That's it," she said. She struggled to a sitting position, then got to her feet.

"I saw his face." She swayed. The red-headed woman stretched out a muscular arm just a second too late. The girl pitched forward, throwing her hands in front of her. The palms rested against the diamond-shaped plate glass panel of the outer door. The red-headed woman shifted her grip, picked the younger woman up as though she had been a doll, and laid her back on the couch.

"Oh, my God," moaned the young woman.

Mason bent over her, solicitously. "All right?" he asked.

She smiled wanly. "I guess so. I got dizzy when I got up, but I'm all right now."

"This man had one eye?" Mason asked.

"Yes," she said, her voice growing stronger.

"No, no!" Sylvia Basset said, her voice almost a moan.

"Let *her* tell it," Dick Basset said savagely. "Everyone else keep out of it."

"Did he hit you more than once?" Mason asked.

"I think so. I don't remember."

"Do you know whether he went out this front door?"

"No."

"Did you hear him drive away?"

"I don't know, I tell you. He hit me and everything turned black."

"Let her alone, can't you?" Dick Basset said to Perry Mason. "She isn't a witness on the witness stand."

Perry Mason strode toward the door which led to the inner office. He reached his hand to the knob, then hesitated a moment, drew back his hand, and took a handkerchief from his pocket. He wrapped the handkerchief around his fingers before he turned the knob. The door swung slowly inward. The room was just as he had seen it the first time. A light in the ceiling gave a brilliant, but indirect, illumination.

Mason crossed to the door of the inner office. It, too, was closed. Once more he fitted a handkerchief in his hand and turned the knob. The room was dark.

"Anyone know where the light switch is here?" Mason asked.

"I do," Mrs. Basset said. She entered the room, and, a moment later, the lights clicked on.

Mrs. Basset gave a half scream of startled terror. Perry Mason, standing in the doorway, stiffened to immobility. Dick Basset exclaimed, "Good God! What's that?"

Hartley Basset lay face down on the floor. A blanket and a quilt, folded together, partially covered his head. His arms were outstretched. The right hand was tightly closed. A pool of red had seeped out from his head, soaked up by the blanket and quilt on the one side and the carpet on the other. A portable typewriter was on the desk in front of him, and a sheet of paper was in the machine, approximately half of it being covered by typewritten lines.

"Keep back, everyone," Perry Mason said. "Don't touch anything."

He stepped cautiously forward, keeping his hands behind his back. He bent over the corpse and read the paper which was in the typewriter.

"This," he said, "seems to be a suicide note. But it can't be suicide, because there's no gun here."

"Read it aloud," Dick Basset said in an excited voice. "Let's hear what's in the note. What reason does he give for committing suicide?"

Perry Mason read in a low monotone:

"I am going to end it all. I am a failure. I have made money, but I have lost the respect of all of my associates. I have never been able to make friends or to hold friends. Now I find that I cannot even hold the respect and love or even the friendship of my own wife. The young man who is supposed to be my son and has taken my name hates me bitterly. I have suddenly come to the realization that no matter how self-sufficient a man may think he is, he cannot stand alone. The time comes when he realizes that he must be surrounded by those who care something for him if he is going to be able to exist. I am a rich man in money, and a bankrupt in love. Recently something has happened which I do not need to put on paper, but which convinces me of the futility of trying to hold the love of the woman who is the dearest thing in the world to me. I have, therefore, decided to end it all, if I can get nerve enough to pull the trigger. If I can get nerve enough . . . if I can get nerve enough . . ."

"He's got something in his hand," Dick Basset said.

Perry Mason leaned down, hesitated a moment, then pried the fingers slightly apart.

A glass eye, clutched in the dead hand, stared redly at them, unwinking, evil.

Mrs. Basset gasped.

Perry Mason whirled to her.

"What does that eye mean to you?" he asked.

"N-n-n-nothing."

"Come on. Come clean. What does it mean to you?"

Dick Basset pressed forward. "Look here," he said, "you can't talk to my mother that way."

Mason waved him away with a gesture of his hand.

"Keep out of this," he said. "What does that eye mean to you?"

"Nothing," she said, more defiantly this time.

Mason turned toward the door.

"Well," he said, "I guess there's no further need for my services."

She clutched his sleeve in frenzy.

"Please," she said. "*Please!* You've *got* to see me through this."

"Are you going to tell me the truth?"

"Yes," she said, "but not now—not here."

Dick Basset moved toward the dead man.

"I want to see," he said, "what . . ."

Perry Mason took his shoulder, spun him around, and pushed him out through the door.

"Turn out the lights, Mrs. Basset," he said.

She switched out the lights. "Oh, I've dropped my handkerchief," she said. "Does it make any difference?"

"You bet it makes a difference," Perry Mason said. "Get your handkerchief and get out."

She groped around for a few moments. Perry Mason stood impatiently in the doorway. She came toward him.

"I have it," she breathed, clinging to his arm. "You must protect me, and we've both got to protect Dick. Tell me . . ."

He broke away from her, jerked the door closed behind them, and crossed the other office to the entrance room.

The woman who had been on the couch was now standing. Her face was dead white. Her lips made an attempt at a smile. Mason faced her.

"Do you know what's in there?" he asked.

"Is it Mr. Basset?" she half whispered.

"Yes," Perry Mason said. "You saw the man who came out of the room clearly?"

"Yes."

"Did he see you? Would *he* know *your* face if he saw you again?"

"I don't think so. I was in the dark here in the room. The light was coming from that other office. It streamed on his face. I had my back turned to it. My face was in the shadow."

"He wore this mask?"

"Yes. That's it. It's carbon paper, isn't it?"

"You saw one eye socket that was vacant?"

"Yes, it was awful. The mask was black, you see, and looking through the mask that way with only one eye staring out, and the other a reddish socket. It . . ."

"Look here," Perry Mason said, "the police are coming here. They're going to question you. Then they'll hold you as a material witness. You want to help Dick, don't you?"

"Yes, of course."

"All right. I want to go over this thing in detail *before* the police talk with you. Do you feel well enough to ride in a car?"

"Yes, I do now. I was groggy at first."

"Can you drive a car?"

"Yes."

He took a key from his pocket, tossed it to her and strode to the telephone.

"My coupé's out in front," he called over his shoulder. "Get in it and get started. My office is in the Central Utilities Building. I'll have my secretary there by the time you get there."

He didn't wait for a reply, but dialed a number on the telephone. He heard the ringing of the bell, and, a moment later, Della Street's voice saying, in accents thick with sleep, "Yes? What is it, please?"

"Perry Mason," he told her. "Can you get dressed by the time it takes a taxicab to get to your place?"

"I can get something on that will get me past the censors," she said. "It won't be stylish."

"Never mind the style. Throw on the first thing you come to. Wrap a coat around the outside of it. I'm sending a cab. Go to the office. A woman will be there. Her name is . . ."

He called over his shoulder, "What's that girl's name?"

Dick Basset said, "Hazel Fenwick."

"Hazel Fenwick," Perry Mason said. "Take her in the office. See that she doesn't get hysterical. Be friendly. Pour a little whiskey into her, but don't get her drunk. Talk with her and take down what she says in shorthand. Keep her out of sight until I get there."

"When will you get there?" she asked.

"Pretty soon," he told her. "I've got to let a couple of cops ask me some questions."

"What's happened?" she asked.

"You can find out from the girl," he told her.

"Okay, Chief," she said. "You ordering the cab?"

"Yes."

"I'll be downstairs by the time it gets here. Tell the cab driver to pick up the girl in a fur coat who's standing on the sidewalk. I hope no one looks underneath that fur coat."

"They won't," he told her and hung up the receiver.

He called the office of a taxicab company, instructed them to rush a cab to Della Street's house, and then turned to Mrs. Basset.

"Who else knows about this?" he asked.

"About what?"

Mason made a sweeping indication with his arm.

"No one. You discovered it yourself. You were the first one to go near the room . . ."

"No, no," he said, "not about your husband—about the young woman getting a sock on the head. Are there any servants who know about it?"

"Mr. Colemar," she said.

"Is he," Mason asked, "the bald-headed chap with the spectacles who works in your husband's office?"

"Yes."

"How does he happen to know about it?"

"He'd been out to a movie. He saw someone running from the house and then he saw me running around here in the room. He came in to see what was the matter."

"What did you tell him?"

"I told him to go to his room and stay there."

"Did he see the young woman on the couch?"

"No, I didn't let him see her. He was curious. He kept trying to get over close to the couch to see her. He's all right, but he's a gossip and he'd do anything to injure me. My husband and I didn't get along. He sided with my husband."

"Where did he go?" Mason asked.

"To his room, I guess."

The lawyer jerked his head toward Dick Basset.

"Know where it is?"

"Yes."

"Okay, show me."

Dick Basset looked inquiringly at his mother. Mason grabbed him by the shoulder and said, "For God's sake, snap out of it. The police will be here any minute. Get started! Can we get through this way?"

"No," Dick Basset said, "this is a separate part of the house. You'll have to go in the other entrance."

They stepped through the door to the porch, entered the residence part of the house, climbed a flight of stairs, walked down a corridor, and Dick Basset, who had been leading the way, stepped back and to one side as he indicated a closed door from beneath which came a ribbon of light. The lawyer gripped Dick Basset's arm just above the elbow.

"Okay," he said. "Now you go back to your mother, kick out that red-headed servant and get down to brass tacks."

"What do you mean?"

"You know what I mean. Get your stories together in every detail and account for that gun."

"What gun?"

"The one you had, of course," Mason said.

"Will they ask me about that?"

"They may. It has been fired. What did you shoot it at?"

Dick Basset moistened his lips with his tongue and said, "Not today it hadn't. That was yesterday."

"What did you shoot at?"

"A tin can."

"How many shots?"

"One."

"Why only one?"

"Because I hit the can and I quit while my reputation was good."

"Why were you shooting at a can?"

"I was showing off."

"To whom?"

"My wife. She was riding with me."

"You carry a gun, then, all the time?"

"Yes."

"Why?"

"Because Hartley Basset has been such a brute to my mother. I knew a show-down was coming sooner or later."

"Got a permit for that gun?"

"No."

"No one else saw you shoot at the can except your wife?"

"No, that's all. She's the only witness."

Mason jerked his thumb back down the corridor toward the door and said, "Get together with your mother. Make your stories air-tight."

He raised his hand to knock at the panels of the door, hesitated, lowered his hand to the knob, twisted it and jerked the door open. The same narrow-shouldered, bald-headed man whom he had seen in Basset's office earlier in the evening stared at him through huge tortoise-shell glasses, his face showing exasperation. It changed to amazement as he recognized Perry Mason.

"You saw me tonight in Basset's office," Mason said. "I'm Perry Mason, the lawyer. Your name's Colemar, isn't it?"

The expression of irritation returned to Colemar's face. "Don't lawyers knock?" he asked.

Mason started to say something, then checked himself as his eyes, drifting to the dresser, caught sight of the piece of paper on which he had penciled the telephone number of his residence and which he had given to Bertha McLane.

"What's that?" he asked.

"Is it any of your business?"

"Yes."

"It's something I picked up in the hallway," Colemar said.

"When?"

"Just now."

"What part of the hallway?"

"The head of the stairs, right by Mrs. Basset's room, if you must know. But I don't know what right you've got to . . ."

"Forget it," Mason said, stepping forward, picking up the paper and folding it and putting it in his pocket. "You're going to be a witness. I'm a lawyer. I might be able to help you."

"Help *me?*"

"Yes."

Colemar's eyebrows rose in surprise.

"Good heavens," he said, "what am I a witness to, and how can you help me?"

"You saw a woman who had been injured lying on the couch down in Mr. Basset's reception room just a few minutes ago."

"I couldn't tell whether it was a woman or a man. Someone was lying on the couch. *I* thought it was a man, but Edith Brite was standing in front of the couch and Mrs. Basset was *very* anxious that I shouldn't go near the couch. She kept pushing me away. If you're at all interested, you might care to know that I'm going to report the matter to Mr. Basset in the morning. Mrs. Basset has no right in those offices and I have. She had no right to push me away."

"Overpowered you, did she?" Mason asked sarcastically.

"You don't know that Brite woman," Colemar retorted. "She's strong as an ox and she does everything Mrs. Basset tells her to."

"You'd been out?" Mason asked.

"Yes, sir, to a picture show."

"When you came back you saw someone running down the street?"

Colemar straightened with such frosty dignity as can be mustered by a man whose shoulders have been bent over a desk during years of clerical work.

"I did," he said ominously.

Something in his tone caused Mason's eyes to narrow.

"Look here, Colemar," he said, "did you recognize that man?"

"That," Colemar said, "is something which is none of your business. That is something which I shall report to Mr. Basset. I don't wish to seem disrespectful, but I don't know your connection with Mrs. Basset and I don't know what right you have to invade my room without knocking and ask me questions. You said I was going to be a witness. What am I going to be a witness to?"

Mason heard the sound of a siren as a car rounded the corner with screaming tires. He didn't wait to answer Colemar's question but jerked the door open, sprinted down the hallway, took the stairs two at a time, jerked open the door to the porch, and crossed to the other door just as a touring car slid in close to the curb.

Mason shoved the door open. Dick Basset and his mother, engaged in a whispered conversation, jumped guiltily apart.

"Okay," Mason said, "here are the cops. Don't say anything about any trouble either one of you might have had with Hartley Basset. That line isn't going to go over so good under the circumstances. Do you get me?"

Mrs. Basset said slowly, "I get you."

Feet pounded on the porch. Knuckles pounded imperatively against the door.

She opened it, and two broad-shouldered men pushed their way into the room.

"Okay," one of them said. "What's going on here?"

"My husband," Mrs. Basset said, "has just committed suicide."

"That wasn't the way we got it over the radio," one of the men said.

"I'm sorry," she told him. "My son was hysterical. He was laboring under a misunderstanding. He didn't know what had happened."

"Well," one of the men said, "what *has* happened?"

She motioned toward the door.

"How do you know it's suicide?" the other officer asked.

"You can read the note he left in the typewriter."

The men opened the door. One of them produced a flashlight and sent the beam slithering about the room. The other found a light switch, pressed the button and stood staring at the scene which was disclosed as the lights clicked on.

"How long ago did you find him?" he asked.

"About five minutes ago," Perry Mason said, answering the question.

The men turned to him.

"Who are you, buddy?" one of them asked.

The other one gave a sudden start of recognition.

"It's Perry Mason," he said, "the lawyer."

Perry Mason bowed.

"What are *you* doing here?" the first man asked.

"Waiting for you to get done with the formalities in connection with this suicide," Perry Mason said, "so that I can discuss certain matters with Mrs. Basset."

"How did you happen to be here?"

"I came here to see Mr. Basset on business."

"What kind of business?"

"Not that it makes any difference," Perry Mason said, smiling affably, "but it had to do with the affairs of a young man who had been employed by Mr. Basset. There'd been some misunderstanding between them, and I wanted to get it straightened out."

"Humph!" the officer said, and stood staring down at the corpse.

"Anyone hear the pistol shot?"

No one answered.

"Evidently used the blanket and quilt to muffle the pistol shot," the officer said. "There's the gun that did the killing."

Perry Mason followed the direction of his pointing finger. On the floor, in plain sight, lay a gun, a .38 caliber Colt, Police Positive, very apparently the gun which he had taken from young Basset.

One of the officers stepped to the corpse, picked up a corner of the blanket and raised it.

"Say, look here!" he called in an excited voice. "Here's another gun under this blanket. How the devil could a man commit suicide with *two* guns?"

The second officer pushed the spectators toward the doorway.

"Get out of here," he said, "and let me use the telephone. I'm calling the Homicide Squad."

Mason stared at Mrs. Basset.

"*Two* guns," he said.

She made no answer. Her lips were bloodless, her eyes dark with terror.

5

THE WITNESSES SAT IN A HUDDLED GROUP IN THE OUTER office. The members of the Homicide Squad busied themselves in the death chamber.

Perry Mason leaned toward Mrs. Basset.

"What did you mean by planting that gun?" he whispered.

"Will it make trouble?" she asked.

"Of course, it'll make trouble. Why did you do it?"

"Because," she said slowly, "there couldn't have been a suicide, without the gun being found there. I didn't think there was any gun. You know, we couldn't see any when we were in the room. We didn't move the blanket, and . . ."

"But *why*," the lawyer demanded, "did *you* put that gun there?"

"I had to," she said. "There had to be a gun there. Otherwise it wouldn't have looked like suicide. It would have looked like murder."

"Don't ever kid yourself," Mason said grimly, "that it wasn't murder, and that was Dick's gun you left there."

"I know," she said rapidly, "but that's all right. Dick and I fixed that all up. We'll say that Hartley borrowed the gun from him more than a week ago and that Dick hasn't seen it since."

"But," Mason said, "the gun is empty. There couldn't have been a suicide with . . ."

"Oh, no," she said. "I put shells in it before I left it in the room."

"The same shells I took from Dick, including the empty cartridge?"

"Yes."

"Did you ever know," Mason asked, "that the police can tell from an examination of bullets whether a bullet has been fired from a certain gun?"

"No, can they?"

"And did you ever know that the police can develop latent finger-prints on that gun, and that when they do, they will find yours and Dick's and mine?"

"Good God, no!"

"You," Mason told her, "are either one of the cleverest women I've met in a long time, or one of the dumbest."

"I don't know about criminal matters," she said. "I wouldn't know anything about them."

"Look here," Perry Mason said, staring steadily at her, "did you think that Hartley Basset had gone out, or did you *know* that he was lying in there dead?"

"Why, I thought he'd gone out, of course. I tell you I saw him run out. . . . I thought it was he."

"Now this girl is your daughter-in-law?"

"Yes, she married Dick. But you mustn't say anything about that marriage."

"Why not? What's wrong with it?"

"Please," she said, "don't ask all those questions now. I'll tell you later."

"Now, listen," Mason said grimly, "there's going to be a lot of questions asked you tonight. Are you ready to answer them?"

"I don't know. . . . No, I *can't* answer questions."

"Why?"

"Because I don't know what to say."

"When will you know what to say?"

"After I've talked with Dick again. I must talk with him once more."

Mason tapped her knee with his forefinger.

"Did you kill him?" he asked.

"No."

"Did Dick?"

"No."

"Why do you want to talk with Dick then?"

"Because I'm afraid they'll find out who did kill him. . . . Oh, I can't talk about it. Please leave me alone."

"Just one question," Mason said, "and tell me the God's truth. *Did* you kill him?"

"No."

"Can you prove you didn't if it comes to a pinch?"

"Yes. I think so."

"All right. There's only one way to keep the police and the newspaper people from turning you wrong side out. Tell them you are too upset to answer questions. They'll go right ahead and ask them anyway. Then you start in getting hysterical. Tell them anything. Contradict yourself every few minutes. Say you saw your husband an hour before the shooting, then say it was a week before the shooting—that you can't remember having seen him for a month. Make wild statements. Say there were voices that warned him that the serpent said he would be killed.

"In other words act crazy. Let your voice get more and more shrill. Keep telling them absurdities. Make a nuisance of yourself. Scream, shout, laugh, have hysterics. Do you understand?"

"Yes," she said; "I think I do. But won't it be dangerous?"

"Of course, it'll be dangerous, but not half as dangerous as trying to explain things and getting caught in a police trap. Remember now, don't do this unless you're innocent and can prove yourself innocent if it comes to a show-down. And don't be conservative in your statements. Make them sound so absurd you'll seem either drunk or crazy, and throw in a lot of screams and laughter.

"In that way they'll figure you're a nuisance and you'll rate a hypodermic. After they've once drugged you, you play possum. When you wake up, pretend to be groggy. Talk thick. Slur your words together, close your eyes and drop off to sleep between words.

"That'll stall 'em along until I can get a line on . . ."

The door opened. Sergeant Holcomb of the Homicide Squad jerked his head to Perry Mason.

"You," he said.

Mason strolled nonchalantly into the room.

"What do *you* know about this?"

"Nothing very much."

"You never do," Holcomb said wearily. "Suppose you tell us how much 'not very much' is?"

"I came out here," Perry Mason said, "to take up a business matter with Hartley Basset."

"What was the business matter?"

"It related to a matter of accounting between Basset and a former employee."

"Who was the former employee?"

"My client."

"What's his name?"

"I'll have to get his permission before I can tell you that."

"What did you do when you got here?"

"I found a scene of some excitement."

"What was the matter?"

"You'll have to ask the others; I don't know. It seems there'd been some friction between Hartley Basset and his son, Dick Basset, and there was a young lady who had been hurt."

"What had hurt her?"

"Someone had struck her, she said."

"Oh, ho!" Holcomb said. "*Who* struck her?"

"She didn't know."

"How did it happen she didn't know?"

"She'd never seen the man before."

"What became of her?"

"I took the liberty of sending her to a place where she could be quiet until morning."

"You did *what?*"

Perry Mason lit a cigarette and said easily, "Sent her some place where she could be quiet."

"You had a crust, doing that."

"Why?"

"Did you know there was a murder case here?"

Perry Mason raised his eyes and said in surprise, "Good heavens, no!"

"Well, you know it now."

"Why," Mason said, "who was murdered?"

Sergeant Holcomb laughed mockingly.

"For a guy that's been around as much as you have, you have to get hit over the head with a club in order to recognize a murder when you see one."

"Hartley Basset shot himself," Perry Mason said.

"Oh, yeah?" Sergeant Holcomb countered. "*You're* telling *me*, I suppose."

"Didn't he?" Mason inquired.

"He did not."

"But the note that was in his typewriter said he did."

"Anyone can write a note on a typewriter."

"He put a blanket and a quilt around the gun, so as to muffle the sound of the shot."

"Why?" Holcomb asked.

"So as not to disturb the household, I suppose."

"And why didn't he want to disturb the household?"

"Consideration, I suppose."

"Baloney! A man who's committing suicide knows he's going to be discovered. He doesn't care. A man who's committing murder is the one who cares about having an opportunity to get away before he's discovered. And a man who's killing himself doesn't use three guns to do the job with."

"Three guns!" Mason exclaimed.

"Three guns," Sergeant Holcomb said. "One on the floor, in the open, one concealed under the quilt and blanket, one that Basset was carrying in a spring holster under his armpit. And that gun hadn't been disturbed. If Basset had wanted to kill himself, why wouldn't he have used *his* gun, instead of going to the trouble of getting another gun to do the job with?"

"Which gun did the killing?" Mason asked.

Sergeant Holcomb smiled patronizingly.

"Naughty, naughty," he said. "*I'm* asking the questions."

Mason shrugged his shoulders.

"Where did you send this jane that got rapped over the head?"

"Where she could be quiet."

"What place?"

"If I told you the place," Mason said, "it would cease to be a place where she could be quiet."

"Listen," Holcomb said, his voice almost choking with rage, "this is a murder case. Does that mean anything to you?"

"Yes," Perry Mason said; "I think it does."

"You bet it does," Holcomb told him. "We want to question that girl. It may mean discovering the identity of the murderer. Now, you kick through, brother, and tell me where she is, and make it snappy. You've got just one chance."

"She's at my office," Mason told him.

"Why did you send her there?"

"Because I thought she needed an opportunity to collect

herself. At the time, I didn't have an idea Basset had been murdered. I thought, of course, it was suicide."

"And is that very efficient secretary of yours at your office?" Holcomb asked.

"Why, of course," Mason said; "someone had to be there to let the young woman in."

Holcomb's face darkened. "In that way," he said, "*you* get a chance to get a statement from the only material witness before the police even have a chance to question her."

Mason shrugged his shoulders and said evenly, "And if you'd got to her first you'd have locked her up so no one could ever have found out what her story was until she was put on the witness stand. *That* is the way *you* like to play the game. But I assure you, my *dear* Sergeant, I only sent her where she could be quiet because I thought it was a case of suicide. As soon as you told me it was murder, you'll have to admit I gave you her location."

Someone snickered.

Holcomb whirled to one of the men.

"Telephone headquarters," he said, "and tell them to pick up that girl at Perry Mason's office. Smash the doors down if you have to. She's a material witness. Tell them Mason's getting a shorthand report of her story. Give that secretary ten minutes more with her and there won't be any case."

Perry Mason said with dignity, "Have you chaps any *more* questions to ask of me?"

"What time did you get here?" Holcomb inquired.

"Shortly after midnight—perhaps twenty minutes after twelve."

"Basset was dead when you got here?"

"Apparently. I was in the outer office all the time, and I heard no sound from this room. Mrs. Basset went in here to get something, and she discovered the body."

"Did you notify the police?"

"We discovered it just as the police were coming in the door. They'd been summoned in connection with the attack which had been made upon Miss Fenwick."

"Who's Miss Fenwick?"

"The young woman who was attacked."

Sergeant Holcomb stared moodily at Perry Mason.

"Is she your client?"

"No, not at present, anyway."

"Had you ever seen her before?"

"No."

"How did it happen you wasted so much time talking with these people in the outer room?"

"I came out here," Mason said, "to see Basset."

"How did it happen you wasted so much time chewing the fat, if you came out here to see Basset?" Sergeant Holcomb demanded.

"Because there was a lot of excitement in connection with the attack on the young woman, and I suggested the police be summoned."

Holcomb said, "That's the second time you've mentioned about the police and both times you've said the police were to be sent for, or words to that effect."

Mason exhaled cigarette smoke, and said nothing.

"You keep putting it that way," Holcomb went on, "which is a funny way of expressing it. Now then, I'm going to get to the bottom of this. Never mind telling me the police were sent for, but tell me *who sent for the police?*"

"I did."

"Did you tell them who you were?"

"No; I told them I was young Basset."

"Why did you tell them that?"

"Because I wanted to get some action. I was afraid they'd think it was a stall if I told them who was talking, and I didn't have time to make a lot of explanations."

Sergeant Holcomb sighed wearily. "You win," he said; "you always have an answer." He waved his hand toward the door. "Okay, you can go now. And if you think you can get to your office before the boys from headquarters do, you're just an optimist, that's all."

"I'm in no particular hurry," Mason said.

"Oh, yes, you are," Sergeant Holcomb told him. "You're on your way right now. You're a busy man, Mr. Mason, and you came here just to see Mr. Basset on a matter of business. Mr. Basset is dead, so you can't see him about any business. Therefore, you've got nothing to talk to anyone about. You haven't been retained by anyone here. You didn't know Mr. Basset was murdered. You thought it was a suicide. And the young woman who was attacked isn't here any more, so there's nothing to hold you here and we're not going to interfere with your sleep. You can go on your way *right now*."

"I can at least wait while I telephone for a taxicab," Mason said.

Sergeant Holcomb grinned.

"Your car isn't here?"

"No."

"What happened to it?"

"I told the young woman to take it up to my office."

"What were you intending to do—about getting up to your office?"

"I was going in a taxicab."

"Well, well, well," Sergeant Holcomb said. "That's too bad. We can't have the leading trial lawyer of our city waiting around while we get taxicabs. Good Lord, no. His time's too valuable. One of you boys put him in a police car and take him up to his office. See that he gets delivered right away and without any delay, and bring Mrs. Basset in here, before he goes, and we'll find out what *she* knows about this."

Perry Mason ground out his cigarette in an ash tray.

"For a man who gets as few real results as you do, Sergeant, you're remarkably cunning in your methods."

And the lawyer bowed his way out while Sergeant Holcomb was trying to think up an answer.

6

PERRY MASON UNLOCKED HIS PRIVATE OFFICE, SWITCHED ON the lights, and walked through the suite until he came to the entrance room, the door of which bore the words:

PERRY MASON
LAWYER
Entrance

Della Street, seated behind a desk reading a law book, looked up at him with a grin.

"I'm studying law, Chief," she said.

She wore a fur coat which buttoned tightly about her. A length of stockinged leg protruded through the opening in the fur coat.

"The police been here?" the lawyer asked.

"I'll say. They did a lot of wisecracking."

Mason's face clouded.

"Did they get rough with the girl?" he asked.

She let her eyes get wide.

"Why, I thought you ditched the girl some place. She didn't show up."

"She didn't show up here?" Mason inquired.

Della Street shook her head.

"What did you tell the cops?" he asked.

"They cracked wise," she told him, "and I cracked wise back at them. I figured you'd found out the police were coming here, so you'd ditched the girl. That gave me a chance to be sassy. I told them I'd just dropped in to study a little; that I did a lot of night studying because you wanted me to become a detective; that you said *so* many of the detectives were incompetent there should be lots of room for a real intelligent one."

"How soon did you get here?"

"The cab was at my place in about two minutes after I hung up the phone. I was down on the street waiting. I gave him a tip to make a fast run. We got here in nothing flat. I came in and switched on the lights in this room, and left the door unlocked. I also told the night watchman that a young woman was coming up to the office, and to see that she got here if she made any inquiries."

Perry Mason gave a low whistle.

"Paul Drake was looking for you," she said. "The watchman told him I was in when Paul started home. So he came back to the office and left a package for you." She indicated a pasteboard package on the table, tied with string and sealed in several places with red sealing wax.

The lawyer took out his knife, slit the string, and said, "Did you have any trouble with the officers?"

"No. I let them look through the whole place. They thought I was holding a woman up my sleeve."

"Hard to convince?" the lawyer asked, lifting the cover from the box.

"No," she said. "They were delightfully easy to convince. They figured it out that you'd told the detectives you'd sent the girl here. Therefore, they figured it was the last place on earth where she'd really be. Not finding her here was not only exactly what they expected, but gave them a chance to make their wisecracks."

Mason lifted the top layer of cotton from the box, took out six bloodshot glass eyes, which he spread on the desk, where they stared up unwinkingly.

"We've got Brunold's address?" he asked.

"Yes. It's in the file."

"Was there a telephone number?"

"I think so. I'll see."

She opened a file of card indexes and pulled out a card.

"Telephone?" he asked.

"Yes. It's here."

"Get him."

She looked at her wrist watch, but Mason said impatiently, "Never mind the time. Go ahead and get him."

She plugged in a line, dialed a number, waited for almost a minute, then said, "Hello, is this Mr. Brunold?"

She glanced across the desk at the lawyer, and nodded.

"Tell him to come up here," Mason said. "No, wait a minute; I'd better tell him myself."

He took the telephone from her and said, "This is Perry Mason talking. I want you to come up to my office right away."

Brunold's voice was sulky.

"Listen," he said. "You haven't any business that's important enough to make me . . ."

"You paid me fifteen hundred dollars," the lawyer said, "because you had confidence in my ability to get you out of a mess. That was before you got in the mess. You're in it now. My best judgment is that you should come up here. If you don't follow my advice you've made a poor guess and thrown away fifteen hundred dollars backing it. I'll be in my office for ten minutes. If you don't stop to shave, you can make it."

Perry Mason dropped the receiver back on the hook without waiting for Brunold to make any further comments.

Della Street looked at him, speculatively, and said, "Is he in a mess?"

"I'll say he is. Hartley Basset was murdered tonight. He was holding a bloodshot glass eye clutched in his hand when they found the body."

"But, does Brunold know Basset?"

"That's what I want to find out."

"He should be in the clear," she said slowly. "He complained of the loss of the eye this morning."

Mason stared at the six bloodshot eyes which glowered so redly up at him, and nodded his head slowly.

"It's a point," he said, "to take into consideration. But don't overlook this fact: Harry McLane worked for Basset. Brunold was acquainted with Harry McLane. Where did Brunold and Harry McLane get acquainted? Did the McLanes come here by accident, or did Brunold send them?"

"Whom are we representing?" she inquired.

"Brunold, for one," he said, "Miss McLane, for another, perhaps Mrs. Basset."

"How was the murder committed?" she asked.

"So it might have looked like a suicide, but it was pretty clumsy. Then Mrs. Basset complicated things by planting a gun. A quilt and a blanket had been used to muffle the sound of the shot. One gun was under them. Mrs. Basset planted a second gun. She *said* it was because she didn't see the first gun, and she wanted the thing to look like a suicide."

"Well?" Della Street asked.

"Well," Mason said, "that *may* have been it, or it *may* have been that she knew the concealed gun hadn't been the one that did the shooting, and she realized the police would check it up by comparing bullets."

"Did she leave finger-prints on the second gun?" Della Street asked.

"Yes," Mason said, "hers and mine."

"Yours!"

"Yes."

"How did yours get on it?"

"I took the gun away from Dick Basset, her son."

"And then gave it to her?"

"Yes."

"Gee, Chief, do you suppose that was a play to get your finger-prints on the gun?"

"I can't tell, yet."

She pursed her lips and whistled silently. After a moment she said, "Can you tell me all about it?"

"I got a call about midnight to rush out to Basset's place. Mrs. Basset told me her son, Dick, was threatening to kill her husband. I stalled around for a while, but she made it sound urgent, so I went.

"When I got there, this Fenwick woman was lying on the couch, apparently unconscious. Mrs. Basset said Hartley Basset had hit her. Dick Basset had a gun. I took the gun. They said the woman was Dick's wife, but the marriage mustn't be mentioned. A red-headed woman about fifty, probably a servant, was putting wet towels on the girl's head. Dick Basset was talking big.

"I figured Mrs. Basset wanted a divorce; that her husband would deny hitting the girl, in a divorce court, but he might have a hard time withstanding the rough treatment of two detectives who wanted the facts, so I put in a call for the cops.

"Then the girl came to, and said Basset hadn't hit her but that a masked man, with an empty eye-socket, had slugged her. She'd pulled off the mask and seen the man's face, but because the room was half dark, and light was coming through the doorway, he hadn't seen hers. She said he was a stranger to her. He socked her. The mask was a piece of black carbon paper with two holes in it for eyes. It had evidently been held in place by putting a hat brim down over it. The Fenwick girl ripped the mask off. The pieces that had been torn out were in Basset's private office on the desk.

"Mrs. Basset claims she saw a man running out of the door and driving away in the Basset car. She claims it was her husband, Hartley Basset.

"Naturally, after the Fenwick girl tells her story, I explore the other room. We find Hartley Basset lying dead, like I've told you. I find a chap by the name of Colemar, a weak-kneed, mouse-like chap, who does Basset's bookkeeping, typing and secretarial work, had been in the place and Mrs. Basset had kicked him out. I thought he might be sore, so I went up to talk with him."

"Did you see him?"

"Yes."

"Was he sore?"

"Plenty. Not so much because she kicked him out as because Basset and his wife didn't get along. He worked for Basset. Therefore, he sided with the boss. All he knew was Basset's side of it, and that's all he wanted to know.

"But when I got in his room I found this piece of paper on his dresser. It's the paper I gave Bertha McLane, with my telephone number on it."

Mason took the paper from his pocket, slowly unfolded it, and dropped it on his desk.

"He said he'd found it in the corridor in front of Mrs. Basset's bedroom."

"Then, Harry McLane must have been out there," Della Street said excitedly.

"Either Harry or Bertha," he said. "Don't forget that it was Bertha to whom I gave it. She *may* have given it to her brother, or someone *may* have given it to Mrs. Basset, or Colemar *may* have been lying, or everyone may have been lying. It's one of those cases."

"The blanket and quilt story sounds phony," the girl told him.

"Hell," Mason said, impatiently, "it *all* sounds phony. I picked this Fenwick girl for a key witness. I knew the cops would sew her up so I'd never see her, once they got their hands on her, so I decided to beat them to it. I figured you'd get a complete interview before the cops had a chance to coach her."

"That eye business," she said, "makes it seem like Brunold."

"It does if the girl is telling the truth," Mason said. "But if she was on the square, why didn't she come here? And the mask business sounds fishy as hell."

"Why?" she asked. "Wouldn't the murderer mask himself?"

"How could a murderer," Mason countered, "enter Basset's office, wearing a mask and holding a gun under a quilt and a blanket? How could he approach Basset, stick the quilt and blanket against Basset's head to muffle the explosion, and pull the trigger, all without Basset putting up a fight?"

"He might have tiptoed," Della Street said.

Mason shook his head moodily.

"Then he wouldn't have needed the mask. Mind you, the gun must have been concealed under the quilt and blanket. From the position of the body, it's almost certain that Basset was taken by surprise and never knew what happened, but was facing the man who fired the shot."

Della Street said slowly, "But there were lots of people in that house who could have entered Basset's office and approached him, carrying a quilt and a blanket, without exciting Basset's suspicion."

"Now," Mason said, "you're getting somewhere. Let's start naming those people."

"Mrs. Basset, for one," she said.

"Right," he told her.

"Dick Basset, for another."

"Check."

"And," she said, "perhaps the girl who was lying on the couch."

Mason nodded his head.

"Anyone else?"

"Not that *I* know of."

"Yes," the lawyer said, "there were the servants. Remember that a servant was bending over the girl on the couch. A servant could very logically carry a quilt and blanket on her arm. She might be making up a bed, stopping, perhaps, to ask Basset a question. . . ." Mason paused for a moment's meditation, then said suddenly, "But you're overlooking the significant point in what you've been telling me."

"What is it?"

"Those persons *only*," he said, "could have *entered* Basset's office carrying the quilt and the blanket without bringing Basset to his feet, because Basset was familiar with their faces. But the person who ran *from* that room had his face covered with a mask. That brings us to a consideration of the mask. It had been prepared in a hurry. The carbon paper was probably right on Basset's desk. The man picked it up. . . ."

"After the murder!" Della Street exclaimed triumphantly.

"Now you're getting it," he told her. "The mask must have been an afterthought. But the quilt and blanket to muffle the gun weren't. They show premeditated deliberation. The mask shows haste."

"Why should a murderer mask himself *after* he'd committed a crime?" she asked.

"To get away, of course. The Fenwick girl saw a man sitting in Basset's office. His back was toward her. Basset told her to wait. She was sitting in the reception room, waiting. The man who was with Basset knew that."

"Then he put on the mask only to enable him to escape," she said.

"Looks that way. But why didn't he go out by the back way? Then he wouldn't have needed a mask. But *if* the man who prepared that mask in the first place was the man who wore it out of the room, *why did he tear out an eye hole for his blind eye?* Why didn't he tear out just the one eye hole?"

She shook her head and said, "That's getting too deep for me. How do you know Basset didn't put up a fight?"

"From the way the body fell, for one thing," he said, "and because he had a gun suspended from a spring shoulder holster under his left armpit. He hadn't gone for that gun."

"Then that makes three guns that were in the room," she said.

"Three guns," he told her, moodily.

"And you don't know yet which one actually did the killing?"

"Ten to one," he told her, "it's the gun that has my fingerprints on it. . . . How long ago did Paul Drake leave?"

"He gave me the eyes after I'd been in the office about ten minutes. It couldn't have been over fifteen minutes ago."

"He'll be down at the Red Lion," Mason said, "having a drink with some of the newspaper chaps. See if you can get him on the telephone."

"Going to report your car as stolen?" she asked.

He shook his head.

"It'll turn up somewhere."

Della Street, who had been whirring the dial of the telephone, said, in her sweetest voice, "A client wishes to speak with Paul Drake. Is he there?"

A moment later she said, "Hello, Paul. Just a minute, the Chief wants to speak with you."

Mason took the telephone.

"Paul," he said, "take a pencil and make a note of this. Hartley Basset—Basset Auto Loan Company—a financier, money lender, and, perhaps, a fence. I want to get every bit of dope on him that you can pick up.

"He committed suicide tonight, and he left a suicide note

in his typewriter. The newspaper boys will have photographs.
I want prints of those photographs. I want the low-down on
Mrs. Basset and her son—a fellow by the name of Dick Basset.
Hartley Basset, by the way, isn't the boy's father. I want to
find out why the kid didn't keep his father's name. Now,
here's another one. Peter Brunold, 3902 Washington Street.
In case you don't know it, he's the man who matches up with
the six eyes you got. I want all the dope on him. I want the
fastest work I can get. I don't care how many men you put
on the job. But get them started. Burn up the wires."

Paul Drake's voice, sounding over the telephone as though
he were about to chuckle, said, "I like the casual way you
mention the fact that it's suicide, Perry. I'm betting five to
one it's murder, and I don't even know the facts."

"Shut up," Mason told him, grinning, "and turn that search-
light mind of yours on something that's going to bring shekels
into the cash register."

He dropped the receiver back into place just as the knob
of the door turned. Pete Brunold pushed his way through the
door. He was puffing, and his forehead was beaded with
perspiration. He glanced at his wrist watch and nodded with
satisfaction.

"Made a record run of it, even if the taxi driver did . . ."

He broke off as he stared at the assortment of eyes on the
desk.

"What are those?" he asked.

"Take a look at them," Mason told him.

Brunold examined the eyes carefully.

"Pretty good," he said. "They're *darn* good."

"Found the original eye yet?" Mason asked casually, as
though he were making preliminary conversation.

Brunold shook his head and stared at Della Street. Della
Street pulled the fur coat about her legs.

"How'd you like to get your eye back?" Mason inquired.

"I'd like it."

Della Street replaced the glass eyes in the box, surreptitiously slid a notebook into position on her knee, crossed her
legs, and started taking notes.

"I think I can get your eye for you," Mason said. "Or, I can tell you how *you* can get it."

"How?"

"All you have to do," Perry Mason said, "is to take a taxi-cab, go to Hartley Basset's house at 9682 Franklin Street. You'll find some police there. Tell them that you think your eye is in the place and you want to identify it. They'll take you into a room. Hartley Basset will be lying on the floor with a bullet hole in his head. Something is clasped in his right hand. They'll pry the fingers apart. You'll see a bloodshot eye staring up at you from . . ."

Brunold recoiled momentarily, then recovered possession of himself, and picked up a cigarette from the humidor on the desk. The hand which conveyed the match to the cigarette was shaking.

"What makes you think it's *my* eye?"

"It looks like it."

Brunold said slowly, "That's what I was afraid of. Someone stole that eye and left a counterfeit. I wanted to get the original. I was afraid it would show up in some situation that would be like this. This is ghastly. This is simply awful!"

"Surprised?" Mason inquired.

"Of course I'm surprised. . . . Look here, you don't think that I went out there and killed the guy and then stuck my eye in his hand? I couldn't have done it if I'd wanted to. I didn't have the eye. I told you this morning someone had stolen it and left a counterfeit in its place."

"Did you know Hartley Basset?" Mason inquired.

Brunold hesitated, then said, "No, I didn't know him. I'd never met him."

"Know his wife?"

"I've met her—that is . . . Yes, I know her."

"Know the boy?"

"Dick—er—Basset?"

"Yes."

"Well, yes, I'd seen Dick, met him, you know."

"You knew Harry McLane, who had been working for Basset."

"Yes."

"Where'd you meet him—out at Basset's place?"

"Out there. He was acting as assistant secretary and stenographer. I met him—once."

"Didn't he ever introduce you to Basset?"

"No."

"Did you ever see Hartley Basset?"

"No. . . . I never saw him. I knew of him, of course."

"What do you mean by that?"

Brunold fidgeted uncomfortably.

"Look here," he said. "You're not doing this to sweat me, are you? This isn't a third degree stunt? You wouldn't kid me about Basset being dead?"

Perry Mason tapped a cigarette on his thumb-nail.

"Certainly not."

"Well," Brunold said, "I may as well tell you the truth. I knew his wife, quite well—that is, I'd seen her several times."

"How long had you known her?"

"Not very long."

"Was the friendship platonic, or otherwise?"

"Platonic."

"When was the last time you saw her?"

"About two weeks ago, I think."

"If she thought you were drifting away from her," Mason said bluntly, "would she be above building up a case against you?"

Brunold nearly dropped his cigarette. "Good God," he said, "what do you mean?"

"I mean just what I said, Brunold. Suppose that you'd had a fight with Mrs. Basset. Suppose her husband committed suicide. Suppose she thought you were in love with some other woman and thought you were going to leave her. Would it be at all probable that she'd try to make it seem that her husband hadn't committed suicide, but had been murdered, and that you were implicated in the murder?"

"Why?"

"So as to keep you from going with some other woman."

"But there isn't any other woman."

"Did she know that?"

"Yes. . . . That is, no. . . . You understand, there isn't anything between us. . . . She's nothing to me."

"I see," the lawyer said dryly. "When did you first meet Mrs. Basset?"

"About a year ago, I guess."

"And you last saw her about two weeks ago?"

"Yes."

"And you haven't seen her since?"

"No."

"When did you first find out your eye had been stolen?"

"Late last night."

"You don't think you left it some place?"

"Certainly not. A counterfeit was substituted. That means someone must have stolen the eye deliberately."

"Why did they steal it?"

"I don't know."

"Why do you *think* they stole it?"

"I can't tell you that."

"You met Harry McLane out at the Basset residence?"

"I saw him there, yes."

"Know anything about his being short in his accounts?"

Brunold hesitated perceptibly, then said, "Yes. I heard he was."

"Do you know what the exact amount was?"

"Something around four thousand dollars."

"Did you know a young woman by the name of Hazel Fenwick?"

"Fenwick?"

"Yes."

"No."

"Know a man by the name of Arthur Colemar?"

"Yes."

"Ever talk with him?"

"No, but I've seen him."

"Know Basset's chauffeur?"

"I'll say I do. His name's Overton. He's tall and dark-complected. He looks as though he never smiled. What about him?"

"I just wanted to know if you knew him."

"Yes, I know him."

"Know a fat, red-headed woman about fifty, or fifty-two?"

"Yes; that's Edith Brite."

"What does she do?"

"She's sort of a general housekeeper. She's strong as an ox."

"But you've never seen Basset?"

"Not to speak to, no."

"Do these other people know you?"

"What other people?"

"The people you've been describing."

"No. . . . That is, the chauffeur may have seen me."

"How does it happen you've seen those people and know them, but they haven't seen you and don't know you?"

"Sylvia has pointed them out to me."

Mason whirled on him suddenly and jabbed at the front of Brunold's vest with the glowing end of his cigarette.

"Dick Basset," he said, "saw you yesterday."

"Where?"

"At the house."

"He must have been mistaken," Brunold said.

"Then it was Colemar who saw you."

"He couldn't have seen me."

"Why?"

"Because I wasn't in his side of the house."

"What do you mean by that?"

"It's sort of a duplex house. Basset has fixed up one side for his office, the other side for his home. Then, when relations became strained with his wife, Basset started living entirely in his side of the house."

"So you were in Mrs. Basset's side of the house yesterday?"

"Not yesterday, it was the day before."

"Thought you hadn't seen Mrs. Basset for two weeks," Mason said.

Brunold said nothing.

"And Dick Basset had an argument with Hartley Basset about you tonight," the lawyer went on.

"Tonight, when?"

"After you left."

"You're mistaken about that," Brunold said positively; "that was an absolute impossibility."

"Why?"

"Because, before I left . . ."

Mason grinned at him.

Brunold moved belligerently toward the lawyer.

"Damn you!" he said. "Just what are you trying to do?"

"Trying to get the facts," Mason told him.

"Well, you can't browbeat me and trap me as though I was a common crook. You can't . . ."

"I'm not trying to browbeat you," Mason said, "and, as far as being trapped is concerned, you're already trapped. You started to say that before you left there tonight Basset was already dead, didn't you?"

"I didn't say I was there at all this evening."

"No," Mason said, smiling, "you didn't *say* it, but that's a reasonable inference from what you did say."

"You misunderstood what I did say," Brunold told him.

Perry Mason turned to Della Street.

"Have you got it all down—the questions and answers, Della?" he asked.

She looked up and nodded.

Brunold rushed toward Della Street.

"For God's sake! Has everything I've said been taken down? You can't do that. I'll . . ."

Perry Mason's hands clapped down on the man's shoulder.

"You'll do what?" he asked ominously.

Brunold turned to regard him.

"You try any rough stuff with that young lady," Mason said grimly, "and you'll go out of here so fast and so hard you'll skid all the way down the corridor. Now, sit down and cut out all this beating around the bush and tell me the truth."

"Why should I tell you anything?"

"Because before you get done, you're going to want someone to help you. You've got a chance to tell me the truth now. You may not have later on. You may be inside, looking out."

"They've got nothing on me."

"You think they haven't."

"No one except you knows I was out there tonight."

"Mrs. Basset knows it."

"Of course, but she isn't a fool."

"Colemar," Mason said, "saw someone running away from the house. He knows who it was. He won't tell me. Was it you?"

Brunold's jaw sagged. "Recognized him?" he said.

"That's what Colemar claims."

"But he couldn't. He was too far away, and I . . ."

"Then it was you Colemar saw."

"Yes, but I didn't think Colemar could see me. He was across the street. I'd swear I saw him first. I kept my head turned away so he couldn't recognize me."

"What were you running for?"

"I was in a hurry."

"Why?"

"Because I knew Sylvia—Mrs. Basset—had telephoned for you. I didn't want to be anywhere around when you came."

"Look here," Mason said; "could you stand up to a rigid questioning and cross-questioning by the police?"

"Of course, I could."

"You didn't stand up under my questioning very well."

"The police aren't going to question me."

"Why?"

"Because they don't have any idea I'm connected with the Bassets in any way."

"Someone coming," Della Street said.

Shadows hulked on the frosted glass of the door. The knob twisted, the door pushed open. Sergeant Holcomb and two of his men stood on the threshold. They looked over the occupants of the office with wary, watchful eyes. Sergeant Holcomb stepped forward.

"Peter Brunold?" he asked.

Brunold nodded and said belligerently, "What's it to you?"

Sergeant Holcomb grabbed Brunold's shoulder, at the same time flipping back the lapel of his coat, showing his gold badge.

"Nothing," he said, "except that I'm arresting you for the murder of Hartley Basset, and I'm warning you that anything you say may be used against you."

He turned to Perry Mason with a supercilious smile.

"So sorry to interrupt your conference, Mason," he said, "but people have rather a nasty way of disappearing after they've talked with you, and I wanted to get Mr. Brunold before he decided a change of climate would be good for his health."

Perry Mason ground his cigarette end in the ash tray.

"Don't mention it," he said. "Come back again sometime, Sergeant."

Sergeant Holcomb said ominously, "If the district attorney feels the same way I do about what happened to that witness, I will come back. And when I leave here, I won't leave alone."

Perry Mason's manner was urbane.

"Glad to see you any time, Sergeant."

Brunold turned toward Perry Mason, and said, "Look here, Counselor, you've got to . . ."

Holcomb nodded to the two men. They jerked Brunold to the door.

"Oh, no, you don't," Holcomb said. "You've had your little chat."

"You can't keep me from talking with a lawyer," Brunold bellowed.

"Oh, no," Sergeant Holcomb said; "after you've been booked and placed in jail, you've got a right to call for a lawyer—but a lot's going to happen between now and then."

The men pushed Brunold through the door. He hung back and tried to struggle. Handcuffs flashed. Metal clicked. Brunold was jerked forward. "You asked for it," one of the men said.

The door banged shut.

Sergeant Holcomb, left behind, glowered at Perry Mason.

Mason yawned, and covered the yawn with four polite fingers.

"Pardon me, Sergeant," he said, "if I seem to yawn. I've had rather a strenuous day."

Holcomb turned, jerked open the door, paused in the doorway, and said, "For one whose methods are so damned cunning, *you* get rotten results."

He slammed the door.

Mason grinned at Della Street cheerfully.

"How about looking in on one of the late night clubs before you go home?"

She glanced down at herself and said, "If I took this fur coat off I'd be arrested. Remember, you told me to dress in a hurry. This coat covers a multitude of sins."

"Then you're going home," Mason said firmly. "At least one of us should keep out of jail."

Her eyes were worried.

"Chief, you don't mean he's going to get you?"

He shrugged his shoulders, bowed, and held the door open for her.

"One never knows," he said, "just what Sergeant Holcomb *will* do. He's so blunderingly ubiquitous."

7

PERRY MASON, FRESHLY SHAVED, PAUSED AT DELLA STREET'S desk to smile down at her.

"Feeling all right after your late hours?" he asked.

"Like a million," she said. "I see the papers play up Hartley Basset's murder, but say nothing about Brunold."

"The newspaper boys don't know anything about Brunold," he told her.

"Why?"

"Because Holcomb didn't take him down to headquarters. Brunold was taken to some outlying precinct where they could sweat him."

"Wasn't there anything you could do about that?"

"I might have got a *habeas corpus*, but I didn't want to show my hand—yet. I don't know the facts. Brunold may be better in than out. The police would have all they wanted out of him before I could have had the writ issued."

"How about Mrs. Basset?"

"I telephoned her as soon as I got to my apartment."

"Talk with her?"

"No. She staged hysterics after I left. Holcomb couldn't get anywhere with her. The son called a doctor and then he pulled a fast one. He said he was taking her to a hospital, but she didn't show up at any of the hospitals. The boy won't tell *where* she is. He says he'll produce her whenever it's necessary."

"He wouldn't even tell you where she was?"

"No."

"How did it happen Holcomb let him get away with that?"

"Holcomb came rushing up to get Brunold. That left young Basset his chance. He took it. But it's a cinch the dicks were watching the place. *They* know where she is. They may not be letting young Basset know it, but they do."

"Then," she said, "all Dick Basset did was to fix it so you couldn't reach his mother, but the police could. Is that it?"

"That's about the size of it."

"Then Mrs. Basset doesn't know about Brunold's arrest?"

"Probably not."

"When will she find it out?"

"When she comes down to earth and acts human. I told young Basset to have his mother get in touch with me at the earliest moment; that it was a matter of the gravest importance."

"And she hasn't telephoned?"

"No."

"But couldn't you have found her?"

"What's the use? It's a cinch the police have her under surveillance. If I had gone trying to force my way into the case, they'd have had me in a tough spot, and I may not be in any too good a spot as it is."

"Why?"

"My finger-prints may be on that murder gun."

She made little designs on the corner of her shorthand notebook with a sharp pencil.

"This is the most peculiar murder case you ever got mixed up in," she said. "We haven't any clients in this murder case yet—that is, we haven't any retainer, except Brunold's."

He nodded slowly and said, "I wish I had known where I could have reached Bertha McLane last night. She didn't leave us any address, did she?"

"No, only the boy—Harry McLane—and that, I think, is the number of a pool room."

"It probably would be. See if you can get him on the telephone. Ring the number he gave, and see if they can give any other number where we can reach him right away."

She nodded, made a note on her shorthand notebook and asked, "Was there anything else?"

"Yes," he told her, "ring up the Basset residence. Tell Dick Basset I'm still trying to get in touch with his mother and that it's very important. And, by the way, see if you can . . ."

The telephone bell rang. She picked up the receiver, said, "Yes, who is it, please?" listened a moment, then cupped her hand over the mouthpiece and stared at Perry Mason with eyes that held a glint of amusement.

"Know where your car was found?" she inquired.

"No. Where?"

"Parked in front of the police station. The traffic department's on the line. They say the car has been in front of a fire plug ever since two o'clock this morning. They're inquiring whether it had been stolen."

Perry Mason winced.

"That," he said, "is once they've got me dead to rights. Tell them no, that the car wasn't stolen, that I must have inadvertently left it parked in front of the fire plug."

She took her hand away from the mouthpiece, passed the

information into the telephone, then once more cupped her hand over the mouthpiece.

"And," she said, "it's in a twenty minute parking zone. They've been putting tags on the car at twenty minute intervals ever since nine o'clock this morning."

Mason said, "Give one of the boys a blank check. Send him down to square the thing and pick up the car. Tell him not to do any talking. Can you imagine the crust of the little devil? Taking the car down and parking it directly in front of the police station!"

"Do you think she did it, or do you think the cops picked her up and had her drive down to the station?"

"I don't know."

"If they did," Della Street went on, "it's a great joke on you, because they parked it in front of a fire plug and in a twenty minute parking zone, knowing that you wouldn't dare to claim the car had been stolen—not after you gave the girl permission to drive it away."

He nodded and strode toward his private office.

"It's all right," he said. "Let them laugh. The bird who laughs last is the one who laughs longest. . . . Have you got those eyes?"

"You mean the eyes that Paul Drake had for us?"

"Yes."

She opened a drawer in her desk and took out the box of eyes.

"It sure gave me the willies," she said, "to look at them."

Mason opened the box, picked up a couple of eyes, slipped each into a vest pocket and said, "Put the other four in the safe. Keep them locked up where no one else can find them. These eyes are just a little secret that you and I are going to share between us."

"What are you going to do with them?"

"I don't know. It depends on what Brunold's next move is."

"What *should* his next move be?"

"Telephone me and ask me to act as his lawyer on the murder charge."

Her forehead showed a pucker of worry.

"How about the way you're getting mixed into this, Chief?" she inquired solicitously. "Will Sergeant Holcomb be back with a warrant?"

"Not unless they identify my finger-prints on the gun, and they can't do that until after they've taken my finger-prints. They haven't any record of them down at headquarters. They'll probably be peeved about Hazel Fenwick disappearing, but they won't have anything to pin a charge on. We've got a new district attorney now, and I think he's inclined to be a square-shooter. He wants to get convictions when he's certain he's prosecuting guilty people, but he doesn't want to convict innocent ones."

"You want me to write up the things Brunold said last night?"

He shook his head as he passed into his inner office.

"No," he called over his shoulder, "let that go. We'll see whom we're representing before we take any definite steps." He dropped into his big swivel chair, picked up the newspaper and was reading the account of Basset's murder when the telephone rang and Della Street said, "I got Harry McLane on the telephone. He was very independent, but I got a number out of him where I could talk with his sister. I talked with her, and she says that she must see you right away. She's bringing her brother with her, if she can get him to come. She said that she'd wait all day in your reception room if she had to, but that she simply *had* to see you."

"Did she say what about?" he asked.

"No, she didn't say. . . . I've sent one of the boys down to pick up your car. Paul Drake telephoned and wants to see you at your convenience."

"Tell Paul to come on in," Mason said. "Let me know as soon as Bertha McLane gets here. If the police haven't got the Fenwick girl, she'll probably call up sometime today. She may use a phony name. So if any mysterious woman tries to get in touch with me, be sure that you take the message and get the lowdown on it. You can be tactful but insistent.

"Tell Paul Drake to come directly to my private office. I'll let him in. When I buzz for you, come in and take notes."

He slipped the receiver back into place, read half a column in the newspaper, and then heard a tapping on the door which led to the corridor. He opened it, and Paul Drake, his face set in its fixed expression of droll humor, entered the room.

Mason looked at him shrewdly and said, "You look as though you'd had a good night's sleep last night."

"Well," Paul Drake told him, "I got darn near twenty minutes."

"Where did you get it?" Mason asked, pressing the buzzer summoning Della Street.

"In the barber's chair this morning. I wish you'd get your brainstorms during office hours. You always want your rush stuff put through at night."

"I can't help it," Perry Mason told him, "if murderers insist on claiming their victims after office hours. Did you find out anything?"

"I found out lots," Drake said. "I had twenty operatives working on the thing at one time, chasing down different angles. I hope you've got a client with long purse strings."

"I haven't, but I'm going to have. What's the dirt?"

"It's quite a story," Drake told him; "one of those human interest yarns."

Mason indicated the big over-stuffed leather chair.

"Sit down and spill it."

Paul Drake jack-knifed his long length into the chair, sliding around and sitting sideways, so that his back rested against one of the arms, while his knees draped over the other arm. Della Street came in, smiled at the detective and sat down.

"It goes back to one of these romantic betrayals of the mid-Victorian Era."

"Meaning what?"

Drake lit a cigarette, puffed out a cloud of smoke, waved his hand in an inclusive gesture and said, "Picture to yourself a beautiful farming community, prosperous, happy and narrow-minded—accent on the narrow-minded."

"Why the accent?" Mason inquired.

"Because it was that sort of a community. Everyone knew what everyone else did. If a girl turned out in a new dress, there were a dozen different tongues to wag in speculation on where she got it."

"And a fur coat?" the lawyer asked.

Paul Drake threw up his hands in a gesture of mock dismay and said, "Oh, my God! Why blacken a girl's character that way?"

Mason chuckled and said, "Go on."

"A girl lived there named Sylvia Berkley—rather a pretty girl—trusting, simple, straight-forward, clear-eyed."

"Why all the niceties of description?" the lawyer asked.

"Because," Drake said seriously, "I'm for that kid in a big way. I've got a description of her. I've even got photographs."

He searched in his pocket, brought out an envelope, took from it a photograph and handed it over to Perry Mason. "If you think it didn't take engineering to dig out that photograph at four o'clock in the morning, you've got another think coming."

"Where did you get it?"

"From the local paper."

"She made the headlines then?"

"Yes; she disappeared."

"Abducted, or something?"

"No one ever found out. She just disappeared."

The lawyer looked searchingly at the detective and said, "You've got the story behind that disappearance, haven't you?"

"Yes."

"All right, go ahead and tell it to me."

"If I seem to get romantic or poetic or something, it's because I've been up all night," Drake told him.

"Never mind that; get down to brass tacks."

"There was a traveling man who was selling dry goods. His name was Pete Brunold."

"He had one eye?" Mason inquired.

"No, he had two eyes at that time. He picked up his artificial eye later on. That's one of the reasons I'm a little mushy about them."

"Where does it start?" Mason asked.

"I guess it starts with Sylvia Basset's folks. They had ideas. You know, the type that stood so straight they leaned over backwards. Traveling salesmen were slickers from the city. When Brunold started to take the girl out, the folks hit the ceiling.

"There was a little movie house in the burg. You know, there weren't any radios in those days. The movies were just graduating from the galloping cowboy stuff. The town wasn't big enough to get many of the old stock melodramas, and . . ."

"Forget the community," Mason said impatiently. "Did Brunold marry her?"

Drake, in his slow drawl, said, "I can't forget the community without forgetting the story. No, he didn't marry her, and, brother, this is my yarn and I'm going to stick to it."

The lawyer sighed, gave Della Street a half humorous glance and said, "Okay, go ahead with the lecture."

"Well, you know how a high-strung girl does things. The town thought she was going to hell fast. Her folks wanted her to give Brunold the bum's rush. She stuck up for him, and I guess perhaps she had ideas buzzing around in her bonnet— ideas of living her own life. You know, Perry, it was along about that time that girls were just commencing to break away from the kind of stuff that had been drilled into their noodles for generations."

Perry Mason yawned ostentatiously.

"Oh, hell," the detective said, "you're taking all the romance out of my young life—just when I was beginning to think my youth hadn't entirely vanished."

"It isn't youthful romance, it's the mush of senility," Mason said. "For God's sake, get it through your head that I've got a murder case on my hands and I want facts. You give me the facts and I'll hang plenty of romance on them when I dish them out to the jury."

"The hell of it is," Drake said, turning to Della Street, "that when the Chief gets this sketch he's going to feel just the same way about it I do. He's like a bride's biscuit—he puts up a hard-boiled exterior, but when you bust through him he's all soft and mushy on the inside."

"Half-baked is the word you're groping for," Mason told him. "Come on, Paul; let's have the stuff."

"One day," Drake said, "Brunold got a letter from Sylvia. That letter told him they couldn't put off getting married any longer."

The half quizzical smile faded from Perry Mason's face. The impatience left his eyes. His voice showed quick sympathy.

"Like that?" he asked.

"Like that," the detective said.

"What did Brunold do?"

"Brunold got the letter okay."

"And ducked out?" Mason asked, in cold, hard accents.

"No, he didn't. It was a small burg and he didn't dare to send a telegram because he didn't want the telegraph operator to know anything, but he hopped a train and started for Sylvia. That's where fate took a hand. Those were the days when railroad beds were like you found them. My God, I can remember one time when I took a trip on one of those hick lines that I tossed around in an upper berth like a bunch of popcorn in a corn popper on a hot stove. . . ."

"The train was wrecked," the lawyer interrupted. "I suppose Brunold was hurt."

"Cracked his dome, punctured his eye, and gave him a loss of memory. The doctors took the eye out, put him in a hospital and gave him a nurse. I found the hospital records and was lucky enough to locate the nurse. She remembered the case because when Brunold got his memory back he surmised something of what must have been in the back of his mind.

"He put in a person-to-person call for Sylvia and got a report back that Sylvia had disappeared. Brunold was like a crazy man. He had a relapse and was delirious. He talked in his delirium. The nurse figured it was a professional secret and she wouldn't tell me much, but I think she knew."

"Sylvia?" Mason asked, and there was no longer any banter in his tone.

"Sylvia," the detective said, "had been fed up for months with stories about the city slickers, about the women who paid and paid and paid. It was the age of literature that got fat on putting erring daughters out in snow storms. Sylvia's parents had been good at dishing out this sort of dope. When Brunold didn't show up, Sylvia figured there was just one reason. So she busted her little savings bank and beat it. No one knew how she left town. There was a little junction on another road three miles away. The kid must have hoofed it and got a milk train. She went to the city."

"How do you know?" Mason asked.

"I got a break," Drake told him. "I'd like to make you think it was just high-class detective work, but when she got married, and in connection with the boy's adoption, she gave some data that enabled me to check back."

"She married Basset?" Mason asked.

"That's right. She came to the city and took the name of Sylvia Loring. She worked as a stenographer as long as she could. After the child was born she went back to the office. They'd held the place open for her. She worked there for years. The boy kept getting more and more of an expense. He needed an education. She met Hartley Basset. He was a client in the law office. His intentions were honorable. She didn't love him—at least I don't figure it that way. She'd never loved anyone except Brunold. She figured Brunold had taken a walk-out powder, so she was off of men."

"And she made Basset adopt the boy?"

"That's right; she didn't marry him until he'd legally adopted the boy. The boy took Basset's name and apparently proceeded to hate his step-father with a bitter hatred, probably because of the way Basset treated Sylvia."

"What was wrong with it?" Mason asked.

"All I know is servants' gossip," Drake said, "but servants' gossip can be pretty reliable at times. Basset was a bachelor.

He hadn't been an easy man to work for. His idea of marriage was that a wife was a species of ornament in public and a servant in private."

"And," Mason said slowly, "by reason of the adoption, Dick Basset would have inherited a share of Hartley Basset's property."

Drake nodded his head slowly and said, "That's the way Edith Brite figures it. She's a housekeeper. Only she doesn't figure there was any idea of gain in connection with it. She feels the boy was doing his mother a good turn."

"She thinks Dick killed him?" the lawyer asked.

"That's right. I had to get her crocked, but when she got *in vino veritas* she babbled a lot. Sylvia had been through hell. The boy knew it. Hartley Basset was just one of those things. She thinks the boy bumped him off."

Della Street said, "Wait a minute, Paul, you haven't finished with the romance. How about Brunold? Did he find her or did she find him?"

"He found her. He'd been searching ever since he left the hospital. He didn't know how to go about such things and for a while Sylvia had kept herself pretty much under cover."

Perry Mason hooked his thumbs through the arm holes of his vest and started pacing the floor.

"Did Dick know Brunold had found his mother and know who Brunold was?" he asked.

Drake shrugged his shoulders. "I'm a detective," he said, "not a mind reader. Your guess is as good as mine. Apparently Sylvia Basset figured she'd made her bed and was going to lie in it. Brunold wanted her to leave, that's a cinch. The fact that she didn't walk out right then and there shows that something was holding her. From the slant I can get on Hartley Basset's character, it may have been his threat to set aside the adoption proceedings on the ground of fraud, brand Dick as illegitimate, make a big stink generally. Or it may have been that he wouldn't give her a divorce and she wouldn't join Brunold unless she could marry him, on account of the kid."

Mason, still pacing the floor, said, "Where's Mrs. Basset now?"

"She ducked out and went to a hotel somewhere."

"See if you can find her," Mason said. "You shouldn't have any great difficulty. She's the type who would go to one of the better class hotels. There weren't a great number of unescorted women who registered at the better class hotels after midnight last night. You've got pictures of her, I presume."

"Oh, sure."

"All right, run her down."

"This other stuff going to help you?" Drake asked.

"Very much, I think," Mason told him.

A buzzer gave the signal that Della Street was wanted in the outer office. She glanced at Mason, who nodded.

"Were the eyes okay?" Paul Drake asked.

"I think they'll do the work all right, although I'm afraid we got them a little late."

"I was wondering about that when I heard about the blood-shot eye that was clutched in Hartley Basset's right hand."

Mason said cheerfully, "Oh, well, it'll all come out in the wash."

Drake uncoiled himself from the chair and moved toward the exit door.

"You don't want anything else except putting a finger on Sylvia Basset, is that right?"

"That's all for the present. And that was good work, Paul, tracing that stuff down with the limited time you had."

"There wasn't so much of it," the detective said, "except a lot of detail work. The newspaper men had pumped the servants dry. Brunold had left a wide open trail. It was a cinch to chase him down, and, in the adoption proceedings, Sylvia Basset had given the true date and location of the boy's birth. By that time, I guess, she figured it didn't matter much. It happened that I was able to locate the doctor, and the doctor put me in touch with the nurse. The nurse remembered that there had been a pile of love letters, tied with the conventional ribbon, in the girl's suitcase. They'd been addressed to

Sylvia Berkley, and she'd read of the disappearance of Sylvia Berkley in the newspapers."

"And kept her mouth shut?" Mason inquired.

The detective nodded. "Nurses," he said, "see quite a few of those cases. They don't see as many of them now as they did twenty years ago."

"Has she ever got in touch with her folks?" Mason asked.

"I don't know. I haven't been able to find that out."

"Are her folks living?"

"I'll have the dope on that this afternoon. I didn't know just how much attention you wanted to attract, so I'm making my inquiries about them in rather a round-about manner."

"Good work, Paul," the lawyer said.

The door from the outer office opened and Della Street walked through, closing the door carefully behind her. She went to Perry Mason's desk and stood waiting.

The detective said, "Okay, Perry, I'll get that stuff for you early this afternoon. If I get the party located in one of the hotels, I'll give you a ring. I should be able to cover the principal ones within the next half hour."

He opened the door and took the precaution of thrusting out his head and looking up and down the corridor before he stepped out into the hallway, letting the door click shut behind him.

Perry Mason turned to Della Street.

"Well?" he asked.

"You've got to help them," she said.

"You mean Brunold and Mrs. Basset?"

"Yes."

"We don't know the facts yet."

"You mean about the murder?"

"Yes."

"Apparently," Della Street said slowly, "she's never had the breaks. The cards in life have been stacked against her. Why not give her a break now?"

"Perhaps I will," Mason said slowly, and then added, "if she'll let me."

Della Street motioned toward the outer office.

"The McLanes are out there," she said.

"Harry and his sister?"

"Yes."

Mason nodded his head. "Show them in, Della."

8

BERTHA MCLANE STARTED TALKING BEFORE PERRY MASON had said more than a courteous "Good morning."

"We read about it in the papers. Is it going to make any difference?"

"It will make this much difference," Mason said slowly; "the estate will be handled by an administrator or an executor. If Sylvia Basset handles the estate, she'll be friendly. If some other person handles it, the probabilities are there will be trouble. We can't square it now. If there should be a will contest, or something, and a temporary executor should discover the shortage . . ."

Her eyes had grown wider as he talked. Now she interrupted him, saying, "Good heavens, don't you know what happened?"

Perry Mason stopped talking and stared steadily at her. "What happened?" he asked, his voice and manner wary.

She turned to the boy.

"Tell him, Harry."

Harry McLane said, "I paid him off."

Mason stared thoughtfully at the boy.

"Did what?"

"Paid him off."

"Paid who off?"

"Hartley Basset."

"How much?"

"Every damned cent—three thousand nine hundred and forty-two dollars and sixty-three cents."

"Did you," asked Perry Mason, "get a receipt?"

"I didn't need a receipt. I got back the forged notes. That was all the receipt I needed."

"When did you pay him off?"

"Last night."

"At exactly what time?"

"I don't know. It was around eleven o'clock, I guess, or perhaps a little later."

Mason tried to hold the boy's eyes, but McLane looked toward his sister, then out of the window.

"It's all okay now," he said. "We just thought we'd let you know. Come on, Sis, I guess there's nothing else we can do here."

"Wait a minute," Mason said. "*Look* at me."

Young McLane turned his eyes to the lawyer.

"Now keep looking at me," Mason said. "Don't move your eyes from mine. Now tell me. You read the newspapers this morning?"

"Yes, that's why we came here—to find out if it would make any difference."

"Just how long," the lawyer asked slowly, "before Hartley Basset was murdered did you pay that money to him?"

"I don't know, because I don't know when he was murdered."

"Suppose that he was murdered at around midnight?"

"I must have paid it to him a little while before he was murdered, then. . . . Maybe someone stole the money from him."

"You paid him in cash?"

"Cold, hard cash."

"Where did you get the money?"

"That's my business."

"Did you win it gambling?"

"What do you care where I got it? It isn't important."

"It may," Mason told him, "be *very* important. Do you realize that . . . But never mind. Let me ask you a few questions first. Hartley Basset gave you back the forged notes?"

"Yes."

"These forged notes were the only things that he held against you in the line of evidence, is that right?"

"Yes."

"Now, where did he get those forged notes from? In other words, where were they? . . . No, young man, don't look away. Keep your eyes right on mine. . . . Where did Hartley Basset get those forged notes?"

"From a locked note file that he had on his desk."

"Where was the key to that file?"

"On his key ring, of course."

"Do you realize," Mason asked, "that when Basset's body was found and searched there wasn't more than twenty-five dollars in actual currency in his pockets, and that the police haven't discovered any large sum of money either in the safe or in the room where he was murdered?"

"Perhaps," Harry McLane suggested, "the motive of the murder was robbery."

Perry Mason thumped the desk slowly with his fist, giving emphasis to his words.

"Young man," he said slowly, "do you realize that there wasn't anything on God's green earth to have prevented you getting admission to the room where Hartley Basset was working, by telling him that you had come to pay off the money, that, when you were once in that room you could have killed Hartley Basset, that you could have taken the key from Basset's key ring, opened the note file on his desk— a file with which you are thoroughly familiar because of your employment with Basset, taken out those forged notes which represented the only evidence against you, placed a fake suicide note in the typewriter, and left the house . . . No, don't interrupt—and keep looking at me. . . . That the only thing on earth that will prevent you from having to answer questions to the police predicated upon such a theory of what *might* have happened, is an ability to show exactly where you got the money that you paid Hartley Basset and being able to account for your whereabouts at the exact time the murder was committed?"

"Why!" Bertha McLane exclaimed. "You're accusing Harry of murder! Harry wouldn't ever have done . . ."

"Shut up," Mason said, without looking at her. "Let's hear Harry's story first."

Harry jumped up from the chair, turned and walked toward the window.

"Aw, nuts," he called over his shoulder. "You know who killed the old buzzard. You ain't going to make me the goat."

"Come back here," Mason said.

"The hell I will!" McLane said, standing with his back to them, looking out of the window. "I don't have to come back and sit in a chair and let you bore your eyes into mine and frame me, so you can get the breaks for some other client of yours."

"Can you," Mason inquired, his face flushing, "show where you got the money that you paid to Hartley Basset?"

"No. . . . Perhaps I could, but I'm not going to."

"You've got to."

"I don't have to."

"I've got to be able to give the police that evidence, Harry, or they're going to arrest you."

"Let them arrest me, then."

"It's more serious than that. If you can't show that you paid this money and secured legitimate possession of those notes, the police are going to think that you secured possession of them illegally."

"To hell with the police."

"It isn't what the police think; it's what a jury's going to think. Remember, young man, that the evidence would show that you were an embezzler. The prosecution would claim Basset was going to send you to jail—you killed him to keep him from doing so."

"Aw, nuts," Harry McLane said again, but kept looking out of the window.

Mason shrugged his shoulders and turned toward Bertha McLane.

"I'm simply telling you," he said.

"Do the police know about those embezzlements?"

"No, but they will."

Harry McLane turned from the window.

"Listen," he said, "don't let this guy kid you, Sis. He knows who killed Basset, or, if he doesn't, he's a damn fool, but he'd like to make a nice fee for himself putting me on the spot. We're finished with this guy right now. The more you let him talk to me the more of a frame-up he's going to pull on me."

Mason said slowly, "Listen, Harry, you've pulled that line two or three times. You know it's a lie. But if you've got any sense, you must know that you've got to have the answers to these questions before the police find out about you."

"Don't worry about the police," the boy sneered. "You tend to your knitting and I'll tend to mine."

"You paid Basset in cash?" Mason asked.

"Yes."

"What did he do with the cash?"

"Put it in the pig-skin wallet he carries in his coat pocket. You ask his wife about it. She'll tell you he always had the wallet in his pocket."

"It wasn't there when the police found the body, Harry."

"I can't help that. It was there when I paid him the money."

"And you didn't get a receipt?"

"No."

"There was no one present?"

"No, of course not."

"And you can't tell us where you got the money?"

"I can, but I won't."

"Does anyone know that you had that money?"

"That's none of your business."

Perry Mason's telephone rang. He scooped up the receiver. Della Street said, "Paul Drake's on the line. He's got some information that I think you should have."

Mason said, "Yes, Paul. What is it?"

The detective's voice said, "I'm going to talk low, Perry, because I don't want anyone else in the office to hear what I'm telling you, and telephone receivers sometimes play tricks when a chap talks too loud. . . . Now, listen. . . . The police are getting ready to pull a whole bunch of fast ones. They've found out a lot of things. Your man, Brunold, has been spilling information. They've had experts check up on the typewritten note that was in the machine on Basset's desk.

"Now, you know typewriting is just as distinctive as handwriting. The police criminologists say the message on the piece of paper which was in the typewriter on Basset's desk hadn't been written on that typewriter. They've been looking the house over, to find the typewriter that it *was* written on. They located it, in Mrs. Basset's bedroom. It's a Remington Portable that she used for personal correspondence.

"What's more, the experts can tell, by the even impression the letters made, that the thing was written by someone who used a touch system—a professional stenographer. You remember what I told you about Mrs. Basset having been a secretary."

Perry Mason frowned thoughtfully at the telephone transmitter.

"Have you located her yet, Paul?" he asked.

"Not yet, but I picked up this information from one of the boys who had been in touch with a newspaper man. I thought you should have it."

"Yes," Mason said, "I'm glad you gave it to me. Try and locate her just as quickly as you can."

He dropped the receiver back into place and turned to stare moodily at young McLane.

"Harry," he said, "you told me that someone who was very close to Hartley Basset was going to intercede to keep you from going to jail."

"Oh, forget it!" McLane said.

Mason turned to Bertha McLane and said, "I gave you a paper with my telephone number on it—the number of my apartment, where you could reach me after office hours. What did you do with it?"

Harry McLane took a quick step forward and said, "Don't . . ."

"Gave it to Harry," she said.

Harry McLane sighed. "You didn't have to tell him that," he said.

Mason turned back to the young man. "What did you do with it, Harry?"

"Kept it in my pocket for a while."

"And then what?"

"I don't know. Why the hell should I remember all those little things? I threw it away, I guess. I didn't have any more need to call you after I paid the old buzzard off. There wasn't any reason why *I* should carry *your* telephone number around with me. What did you want me to do, seal it up in a pickle jar so it would keep?"

"That piece of paper," Mason said, "was found in the corridor in front of Mrs. Basset's bedroom."

Sheer surprise twisted young McLane's face into a spasm of expression. "It couldn't have been," he said, then, after a moment, with a look of cunning in his eyes, said, "Well, what if it was?"

"When I went out there," Mason went on, entirely disregarding young McLane's comment, "Mrs. Basset tried to intercede for you."

"Did she?" Harry asked tonelessly.

"Did you know she was going to do that?"

"Of course not. I'm not a mind reader."

"Mrs. Basset likes you, Harry?"

"How do I know?"

"Did you see her last night, before you saw Hartley Basset?"

Harry McLane hesitated and said, "Why?"

"You might as well tell me that," Mason said. "The police certainly can find out that much. The servants were in the house and . . ."

"I'm not going to tell you any more about her. Leave her out of it."

"Had you *ever* been in her room?"

"Sure, on business."

"Was there a typewriter in her room?"

"I think so."

"A Remington Portable?"

"I guess so."

"Had you ever used it?"

"Sometimes when I was working there and she had social letters to get out she'd dictate them to me."

"Did Hartley Basset suggest that she do that?"

"I don't know."

"Yes, you do, Harry. Tell us the truth."

"Hartley Basset didn't know anything about it."

"Why did you do it, if it wasn't a part of the duties of your employment?"

"Because she was a good scout and I liked her, and because old Basset was grinding her down."

"So you sympathized with her?"

"Yes."

"And wrote letters for her?"

"Yes, sometimes she'd have neuritis in her right arm."

"Was there a portable typewriter on the desk in front of Hartley Basset when you called on him?"

"Sure. He had his own typewriter there that he makes notes on. Sometimes he dictates stuff and sometimes he pounds it out himself."

"He doesn't have a touch system, does he—just a two-finger hunt-and-peck system?"

"That's all."

"But you have a touch system?"

"Of course."

"Did you know," Perry Mason asked, staring steadily at Harry McLane, "that the note that was found in the typewriter on Basset's desk, stating that he was going to commit suicide, was not, in fact, written on that typewriter at all, but was written on the typewriter which was in Mrs. Basset's room, and that it was written by a professional typist who used the touch system?"

Harry McLane flung himself toward the exit door.

"Come on, Bertha," he said; "let's get the hell out of here."

She got to her feet, stood staring at Perry Mason, then at her brother.

"Harry," she said, "you know Mr. Mason is trying to help you, and . . ."

"Aw, nuts, don't be a sucker. I only came here because you wanted me to. He's looking for a fall guy, I tell you."

Bertha McLane turned to Perry Mason and said, "I'm sorry, Mr. Mason, that Harry feels that way. I hope you'll accept my apology . . ."

"Apology, hell!" Harry McLane interrupted. "Don't be a sucker!"

He pushed his way over toward Mason's desk and said, "You've been asking a lot of questions. Now let *me* ask *you* some. Are you representing Brunold?"

"Yes," Mason said, "I'm representing him. I presume it amounts to that."

"And Mrs. Basset?"

"She has consulted me."

"And Dick Basset?"

"Not directly."

"But through his mother?"

"Perhaps, yes," Mason said, his eyes narrowed to mere slits as he watched McLane's face.

"There you are," McLane said, turning triumphantly to his sister. "Are you going to sit there and let him make a goat of me? I told you we were foolish to come here in the first place."

"Mr. Mason," she said, "can't you . . ."

Harry McLane grabbed her by the arm and pushed her toward the door.

"You claim to care something for me," he said, "but you're putting a rope necktie around my neck if you keep on talking to this bird."

Her face showed conflicting emotions.

Mason said slowly, "Harry, you still haven't told me where you got the money that you claim you used to pay off Hartley Basset. You still haven't told me whether anyone knows you were in possession of that money. You still haven't told me where you were when Basset was murdered, and you haven't told me what was to have kept you from killing Basset, opening the file where the notes were kept and taking out those forged notes."

Harry McLane jerked open the door which led to the corridor. He paused in the doorway to say, "I know enough about legal ethics to know that you can't ever tell anyone anything that I've told you. If you tell the cops that I was out at Basset's place I'll have you disbarred and if you keep your mouth shut I won't have to tell anybody anything."

"But Mrs. Basset," Bertha McLane said, "knows, Harry, that you . . ."

He grabbed her arms and pushed her through the doorway.

"And Colemar knows of that shortage," Mason said, "to say nothing of Mrs. Basset. Don't forget that the police . . ."

"Aw, nuts to you," McLane said, and kicked the door shut.

Mason sat perfectly still, his eyes thoughtful, his fingers still making drumming noises upon the edge of the desk. The telephone rang three times before he changed his position. Then he swung abruptly about in his swivel chair, picked up the receiver and heard Paul Drake's voice saying, "My men have found her, Perry. She's at the Ambassador Hotel, registered under the name of Sylvia Lorton, and there are three police detectives watching her suite. They tailed her there last night. They've also got one of their operatives on duty at the switchboard so they can listen in on any calls that go through the switchboard."

Perry Mason squinted his eyes thoughtfully.

"I presume," he said, "that if I should go over to see her, the detectives would close in on her and make the arrest right now."

"Sure," Paul Drake said cheerfully. "All they're doing is giving her plenty of rope, hoping that she'll hang herself. They'll try to stampede her into making a break if she keeps sitting tight. But, with her son calling her and spilling information over the telephone, the cops will have her where they want her by midnight."

Perry Mason said slowly, "Paul, I've got to see that woman without the police knowing it."

"Not a chance in a million," Drake told him. "You know the game the police are playing as well as I do."

Perry Mason said slowly, "Have you made a check on the location of the fire escapes, Paul?"

"No, I haven't been out there myself. I'm taking reports from a man who's on the ground. Do you want him to do it?"

"No," Mason said. "Get your hat on, Paul, and meet me at the elevator. We're going out together."

The detective groaned and said over the telephone, "I knew you were going to get me in jail sooner or later."

"Any time I get you in," Perry Mason said grimly, "I'll get you out. Get your hat, Paul."

He slammed the receiver back into place.

9

PERRY MASON, ATTIRED IN THE WHITE UNIFORM OF A WINDOW cleaner, a uniform which he had rented at a masquerade costumer's, carried several rubber window-cleaning blades in his right hand. Slightly behind him, Paul Drake, similarly attired, carried a pail of water in each hand.

"I suppose," the detective remarked lugubriously, "you had it all figured out when you arranged for the costumes."

"Had what figured out?" Mason asked.

"That I was to be the assistant, and carry the pails of water."

Mason grinned, but said nothing.

They rode up in the freight elevator to the sixth floor of the Ambassador Hotel. A man, lounging in the corridor, with broad shoulders, square-toed shoes, and a belligerent jaw, eyed them in silent accusation.

The pair ignored the stare, walked purposefully to the end of the corridor, and opened the fire-escape window at the end of the hallway.

"Is he looking?" Perry Mason asked, as he slid a leg out over the window sill.

"Looking in sort of a half-hearted manner," Paul Drake, standing in the corridor, reported. "You've got to work fast."

"Are *you*," asked Perry Mason, "telling *me*?"

He took a sponge from the pail, touched the window over the fire escape, and gently worked the rubber blades which cleaned the window.

"All right," he said; "now for the fast stuff."

"You're certain the room's empty?" asked Drake.

"No," Mason said, "I'm not. We've got to take a chance on that. Stand up close to the door with your back toward it. Knock on the lower panels. Don't let him see that you're knocking."

The lawyer finished putting the polish on the window with a dry rag. Drake said, "Okay. I've knocked twice and got no answer."

"Think you can get it open without too much fumbling around?"

"I think so. Let me study the lock a minute. Okay, I think I've got it. Let's go."

Drake took some keys from his pocket, selected one, inserted it in the door, twisted it into just the right position, put pressure on it, and heard the lock click back. He gave a muttered exclamation of satisfaction, and the two men entered the room.

"The one next to this, on the right?" Mason asked.

"That's right."

"You're sure that's the woman?"

"Virtually certain."

"If it isn't, we're going to be in a jam."

Drake said irritably, "We're going to be in a jam anyway, if we get caught. It's going to be something we can't explain away."

"Forget it," Mason said. "Where's that belt?"

Drake handed him a safety belt. Mason slid out of the window and hooked the belt in an eye placed for that purpose in the wall just outside the window of the adjoining room.

He stood out on the window ledge, caught Drake's hand, steadied himself, and then moved across to the adjoining window, standing for a long moment with his legs spread out across six stories of space.

"Take it easy," Drake cautioned.

Mason slipped the other hook of the belt through the eye on the near side of the window.

"Okay now," he said. "Hand me the water."

Drake stretched out and handed across a pail of water. Mason started sponging the window. A moment later, he knocked on the glass. A woman, attired in underthings, threw a kimono hastily about her shoulders and came to the window, glaring angrily.

Mason made motions indicating that she was to raise the window.

Sylvia Basset flung open the window.

"Look here," she said, "what do you mean by cleaning these windows when I'm dressing? I'm going to complain to the management. You can't . . ."

"Lower your voice," Perry Mason said, "and take it easy."

At the sound of his voice, she started, then her eyes widened with surprise.

"You!" she said.

Perry Mason slid the bucket of water along the ledge.

"Now, listen," he said. "You haven't much time to waste. I want to get the low-down on this thing. Did you know Brunold was arrested?"

"Brunold?" she said, and frowned.

"Yes, Brunold."

"Who is he?"

"Don't you know who he is?"

"No."

"Why did you come here under an assumed name?"

"I wanted to rest."

He nodded toward some bags that were sitting on the floor by the bed.

"Those yours?"

"Yes."

"Did you bring them with you last night?"

"No."

"When did you get them?"

"Dick brought them to me early this morning."

"What's in them?"

"Things."

"You mean you're skipping out?"

"My nerves are all upset. I'm going away for a few days until this thing straightens out."

Mason tightened his lips and said, "You poor little fool, were you trying to take a run-out powder?"

She said, "Well, what if I was?"

"That," he told her, "is exactly what they're trying to get you to do. Flight is an indication of guilt. It's something that can be proved in a case the same as any other fact."

"They'd never catch me—not where I'm going."

"They'd catch you," he said, "before you went there, with a ticket in your pocket."

"Don't fool yourself," she said. "I'd be too smart for that—only I'm not running away. I just don't want . . ."

"Listen," he told her. "There's a police detective in the hall, watching the door of your room. There's another one in the lobby and one at the elevators. The police have put in a special operator at the switchboard. You've been shadowed, your son has been shadowed, and all of your telephone conversations have been overheard. Now . . ."

She clutched her hand to her throat.

"Good heavens!" she exclaimed. "Do you suppose . . . ?"

"Give me the low-down," he interrupted. "What happened after I left?"

"Nothing very much. They asked me a few questions. I had hysterics."

"What did you tell them?"

"I told them the truth at first—that I had wanted to see my husband about a matter of business; that I went into the outer office and found Hazel Fenwick lying on the floor; that I worked with her and brought her to consciousness, and then she told a story of a man with an empty eye socket, running from the room where my husband had his office."

"Did they ask you why you didn't call your husband?"

"I told them that I was so engrossed thinking of Hazel Fenwick, and trying to bring her to consciousness, that I'd forgotten about my husband."

Mason made a grimace of disgust.

"What's wrong with that?"

"Everything," he said. "What happened after that?"

"Then," she said, "they started getting a little nasty and I became hysterical and lied to them."

"What did you lie to them about?"

"Everything. I told them I knew my husband had gone out, and then I told them I knew he hadn't gone out. They asked me if I knew anyone who had an artificial eye, and I told them my husband had an artificial eye. I laughed and screamed, and they called a doctor and I wouldn't let him touch me. I insisted that Dick call my own physician and then when he came out, he sized up the situation and gave me a hypo and sent me to my room."

"Then what?"

"Dick scouted around until he found a back way unguarded and then he came and got me. I was pretty groggy from the hypo, but I managed to walk, keeping an arm on his shoulder. He took me here and put me to bed. I woke up early this morning and telephoned him, using an assumed name so the police wouldn't know who it was—but, if they were listening over the switchboard—my heavens!"

"Did you make any admissions?" Mason asked.

"No. I didn't have anything to admit, except about the hysterics."

"What about the hysterics?"

"He asked me if I'd told the police anything, and I told him no, that my hysterics completely fooled them."

"Anything else?"

"I talked with him two or three times today."

"Make any admissions?"

"Well, I talked pretty freely with him, but I didn't make any damaging admissions."

"Did he?" Mason asked.

"He told me he was glad my husband was dead. Dick had hated him bitterly for some time."

"Now, listen," Mason told her. "You can't stall the police the next time they start questioning you. So you've got to get your story in order. How about the gun?"

"I'll tell them the truth, that I gave it to Dick to protect me with."

"Was that the gun that was used in the killing?"

"I don't know."

"How about Brunold?"

"I don't know any Brunold."

"You should," Mason said. "He's the father of your child."

She clutched at the edge of the table.

"What!" she exclaimed.

Mason nodded and said, "I found out that much through my own detectives. The police can find it out just as easily as I did, providing Brunold hasn't told them already. Brunold has been taken into custody."

"Even Dick doesn't know," she said.

"Does he suspect?"

"I don't think so."

"Brunold was out at the house last night?"

"No."

"Tell me the truth."

"Yes."

"What time did he leave?"

"Do I have to tell the police this?"

"I can't tell yet."

"He left just before I discovered Hazel Fenwick unconscious."

"What were *you* doing in your husband's outer office?"

"I went down there to see if Hazel had fixed things up with Hartley. She had been gone a long time and I was worried."

"Brunold was with you just before you went down?"

"Yes."

"Had he been with you all the time?"

"No, not all the time. I'd gone to my bedroom and left him in my sitting room. I think he stepped into the corridor for something. He wasn't there when I came back, but he came in after a few moments."

"You knew Hazel Fenwick was going down to see your husband?"

"Oh, yes. I wanted her to."

"Was it Brunold's eye your husband was holding in his hand?"

"I think it was."

"How long have you known Hazel Fenwick?"

"Not very long."

"Is there something phony about this Fenwick woman?" Mason asked.

"I can't tell you that."

"You mean you won't. Is there something phony about this marriage to Dick?"

"I don't know. She came to the house for the first time the night of the murder. Dick's Hartley's heir. Hartley wanted to control Dick's marriage. I knew there'd be a scene when he found out. I wanted her to tell him. I thought she'd make a good impression."

"How many at the house knew she was married to Dick?"

"None of them. Overton, the chauffeur, brought her to the house from the station. He thought she was a friend of mine. Edith Brite, the housekeeper, might have suspected, but I don't think so. Those were the only ones at the house who had seen her."

"Did you see Harry McLane last night?"

"No."

"Look here," Mason said; "every once in a while you tell me a lie. It's poor policy to lie to your lawyer. It might put you in a tough spot. Now, did you see Harry McLane last night?"

"No," she said defiantly.

"Do you know if he was out at the house?"

"He might have seen Hartley but I don't think so."

"Someone was in Hartley's office when this Fenwick woman knocked on the door. Who was that?"

"That," she said, "is something I can't understand. I wanted Hazel to have a clear field, so I watched the entrance door and waited until the last client had gone. Then I told Hazel the coast was clear and went as far as the entrance room with her. If someone was in the office with Hartley it must have been someone who came in through the back door."

"Well," Mason said, "did Harry McLane know about the back door?"

"Oh, yes."

"How about Pete Brunold?"

She hesitated a moment and then said slowly, "Pete knew about it, too. That is, sometimes he'd come in my side of the house through the back door. The two back doors are right together. . . . Now you can't say I'm not telling you the truth."

Mason stared at her grimly and said, "I'm not saying *anything*, but I'm doing a lot of thinking. Was Pete Brunold with you all the time he was out at the house the night of the murder?"

"Not all the time."

"Where was he?"

"He thought Overton, the chauffeur, was spying on us. He thought Overton had been snooping around my room, and he went out to try and locate Overton."

"Did he do it?"

"No, he couldn't find Overton anywhere. He said he looked all over the house."

"When was this?"

"Just before I took Hazel down to Hartley's office."

Mason said slowly, "Look here, do you want to protect Pete Brunold or do you want to save *your* skin?"

"I want to protect Pete with my life."

"Don't ever forget," Mason warned her, "that you're in this thing yourself. You can't protect anyone unless you're in the clear, and unless you know and I know exactly what happened. I won't protect Brunold if he's guilty and I won't protect you if you're guilty. Now, Brunold was wandering around the house somewhere about the time the murder was committed. *You* say that he was looking for Overton. He might have met your husband and . . ."

"Look out," Paul Drake said, "just below you, Perry."

Perry Mason started polishing the window, glancing downward beneath his right armpit.

Sergeant Holcomb's frowning face was thrust out of the window directly below.

"This is the blow-off," Mason said. "Tell the police you came here for a rest, that you're ready to go back with them. If you *didn't* kill your husband and want to protect Brunold, refuse to answer any questions. If you want to protect yourself, tell them the God's truth. If Brunold's guilty, he'd better plead guilty. If you *did* kill your husband, and it wasn't justified, get another lawyer. If you're guilty of murder and you lie to me, I'll quit you cold; otherwise I'll stay with you until hell freezes."

"We're innocent," she said frantically. "Pete has been justified . . ."

"Hey, you, up there!" shouted Sergeant Holcomb. "Who told you to wash those windows?"

Mason mumbled an inaudible reply.

"Look around," Holcomb yelled. "I want to get a look at your face."

Mason turned around in such a manner that he kicked the bucket of water over. Sergeant Holcomb saw the water coming, but dodged too late. Some of the liquid splashed in his eyes and face as the bucket hurtled past. He jerked his head back in. Mason grabbed Paul Drake's extended hand, jumped to the adjoining sill, held himself precariously balanced for a moment, then slid down into the room.

"We can," Paul Drake said, "take the fire escape down to the second floor."

"Swell, if they aren't waiting for us at the second floor," the lawyer told him.

The two men opened the door of the room which led to

the corridor. They stepped into the corridor, turned to the left, and through the window which opened on the fire escape. The broad-shouldered detective, still standing in the corridor where he could watch the door of Mrs. Basset's room, glowered at them thoughtfully, took three purposeful steps toward them, and then hesitated.

Perry Mason called to Paul Drake in a loud voice, "Empty the buckets, Paul. We can fill them up from a faucet on the lower floor. We've got to get the rail on this fire escape cleaned up."

Drake nodded. The two men raced down the fire escape. They had gained the second floor, when there was a shout from above them. Sergeant Holcomb appeared on the fire escape, wildly waving his hands.

"Here," Mason said, "is where we take a transfer."

He dove through the open window to the second floor corridor and raced down the corridor. At the head of the stairs he slipped off the white uniform which he had put on over his business suit. Paul Drake, fumbling with a button of the white coveralls, delayed matters somewhat. Mason reached out, ripped off the button, and helped pull the uniform off.

"We've got just one chance," Mason said. "We've got to go up."

He walked to the elevator, the white bundle under his arm, and pressed the "up" button.

"If we have luck," he said, "we can . . ."

A light glowed, a door slid smoothly back. Mason and Drake entered the elevator, just as an adjoining elevator, coming down from the sixth floor, stopped, and its door slid open. Sergeant Holcomb ran into the corridor.

"Floors?" asked the elevator boy, as he slid the door shut.

"Top floor," Mason said.

As the elevator shot upward, Mason said conversationally, "A roof garden, isn't there?"

"Yes, sir."

"Fine," Mason said. "We'll go out there and sit down for a while."

He left the elevator at the top floor, led the way to the roof garden, tossed the white uniforms behind a potted plant, and said, "Have you got that passkey, Paul?"

"Sure."

"Get it ready," Mason said, leading the way to the room corridor.

He picked an inside room, knocked on the door. There was no answer. He nodded to Drake. The detective turned the key in the lock. The door opened, the two men entered, and Mason twisted the knurled brass knob which shot the bolt into position. He took a cigarette case from his pocket, tapped a cigarette on his thumb-nail, and grinned at the detective.

"Well," he said, "we're still out of jail."

"How the devil are we going to get out of this?" Drake asked, his face lugubrious.

Mason stretched out on the bed, pulled up pillows back of his head, blew smoke up toward the ceiling. His face was wreathed in a smile of serene satisfaction.

"They'll think we're playing tag in the corridors," he said. "After a half an hour or so, when they can't find us, they'll think we got down the freight elevator, or took the stairs, and gave them the slip. And, in the meantime . . ."

His voice trailed off into silence.

"In the meantime, what?" Drake inquired.

"I didn't get very much sleep last night," the lawyer said. He took one long, last puff of the cigarette and ground it out in the ash tray. "Call me at six o'clock," he said, "if I'm not awake by then," and closed his eyes.

The detective stared at him in open-mouthed amazement for a moment; then moved toward the couch.

"Hey, you damned hog," he said, "give me one of those pillows. *I* didn't sleep at all."

10

PERRY MASON SPRAWLED HIS SIGNATURE OVER THE PAPER which Della Street handed him, pressed a buzzer, and, when one of his assistants entered the office, said, "Here are all the papers for *habeas corpus* on behalf of one Peter Brunold. Get some fast action."

"You want Brunold out?" the assistant asked.

"They won't let him go," Mason said, "but I want to force their hands and make them put a charge against him. They probably don't want to charge him with murder right now. But that's the only charge they can put against him, so we'll force their hand with a *habeas corpus*."

Mason turned to Della Street, as the assistant took the papers and went out. "Did you ask Drake to come in here?" he inquired.

"Yes. I told him to come directly to your private office. He should be here. . . . That's he at the door now."

A shadow hulked on the frosted glass panel of the door. Della Street glided across the office, opened it, and Paul Drake grinned at Perry Mason.

"Got a hunch?" he asked, sliding into the big over-stuffed leather chair, his knees draped across one of the arms, the small of his back propped against the other.

"Yes," Mason said. "This Fenwick woman."

"What about her?"

"One of three things happened to that woman," Mason said. "Either she was kidnapped by the murderer, or she met with some accident, or she skipped out.

"The murderer didn't know her—that is, he hadn't seen her first. If she'd met with an accident, the police would have spotted her by this time. Therefore, I think she skipped out."

"That, of course," the detective said slowly, "is acting on the assumption she told the truth about what she had seen the night of the murder. She may have skipped out because she knows something that would put Dick Basset on the spot."

Mason nodded his head moodily and said, "There's a diamond-shaped panel of plate glass in the door of Hartley Basset's entrance room. She'd been slugged and was groggy. When she got up from the couch, she staggered and slapped both of her hands against the glass in order to catch herself. She must have left ten perfectly good finger-prints on that glass.

"Now, I'm just wondering about that girl and don't want to overlook any bets. She has some powerful motive for skipping out. Either she's protecting someone, or she's concealing something she did the night of the murder, or she has a record and doesn't dare to stand police questioning. She *could* have gone into the room, found Hartley Basset dead, lifted a bunch of money from his pocket, then socked herself on the head with something and pretended to be out.

"She *could* have seen Dick Basset commit the murder and skipped out to keep from testifying.

"She *could* be a crook, with a criminal record. Let's investigate all the possibilities. Skip out to Basset's house, develop those latent finger-prints on the glass of the door, photograph them, and see if you can get an identification."

Drake nodded slowly. "Anything else?" he asked.

"Not right now. Let's get the low-down on this Fenwick woman."

As Paul Drake turned the knob of the door which led to the corridor, he said, with a droll smile, "There isn't any chance that the cops are right and you have this woman tucked away some place, is there, Perry?"

Mason grinned and said, "You might look under my desk, Paul."

The detective looked puzzled and said, "You son-of-a-gun, if you're sending me on a run-around, I'll never trust you again."

He closed the door, and Mason turned to Della Street.

"Make a note," he said, "to look up how glass eyes are held in place, and how easily they can be jarred loose."

She finished making swift lines in her shorthand notebook, glanced up at Mason and said, "How about your finger-prints on that gun?"

Mason chuckled, and said, "I think the cops have overlooked a bet there. They finger-printed everyone in the house, but they overlooked me."

She asked thoughtfully, "Is Hamilton Burger a shrewd district attorney?"

"I don't know yet," Mason said. "It's too early to tell. This is the first murder case that's come up since he's been in office."

"Do you know him personally?"

"I've met him, that's all."

"If he thinks you're responsible for getting this Fenwick witness out of the jurisdiction of the court, won't he take some action against you?"

"He may."

"What can you do if he does?"

"Simply tell the truth, which won't be enough."

"What do you mean by that?"

"If I told any jury on God's green earth that I had taken the key witness in a murder case, spirited her away from the officers, and sent her up to my office so I could find out exactly what she knew and get a written statement before the officers got hold of her, and then tried to explain that she'd disappeared and I didn't know where she had gone, it would indicate two things to the average newspaper reader: First, that I was a liar; second, that her statement had clinched the case against my client, that I was keeping her under cover for that reason."

Della Street nodded sympathetically.

The buzzer rang the code signal which announced that she was wanted on the telephone for an important message. She glanced at Perry Mason. He nodded. She picked up the receiver and said, "Hello." Her eyes narrowed. She placed her palm over the transmitter.

"Hamilton Burger," she said, "the district attorney, is in the office and wants to see you."

"Is he alone?" Mason asked.

Della Street repeated the interrogation into the transmitter, then nodded her head.

"Bring him in," Mason said. "Stick in here, and be sure that you take down every single word that's said. Perhaps he won't deliberately misquote me, but it's one of those situations where a lot may depend on having an ace in the hole."

She nodded and moved toward the door which led to the outer office. Mason got to his feet and stood straddle-legged, his fists resting on the edge of the desk.

Della Street opened the door and stood to one side. Hamilton Burger, a broad-shouldered, thick-necked individual with a close-cropped mustache, walked into the room and said affably, "Good afternoon, Mason."

Perry Mason nodded cautiously, indicated a chair and said, "Sit down. Is this an official or a social visit?"

"I think it's going to be social," Burger said.

Mason passed him cigarettes. Burger took one, lit up and smiled at Della Street, who had taken up her position at the far end of the desk.

"It won't be necessary to take down what I'm going to say," he said.

Mason said, "It's going to be necessary to take down what I'm *not* going to say, and the only way you can be certain of what I *didn't* say is by having some record of exactly what I *did* say."

The district attorney sized Perry Mason up with speculative eyes and said, "Look here, Mason, I've been checking up on you."

"That's not surprising to me," Mason told him.

"I've found," Burger said, "that you've got a reputation for being tricky."

Mason said, with a trace of belligerence, "Did you come here to discuss my reputation?"

"In a way, yes."

"All right, go ahead and discuss it, but be careful what you say."

"You've got a reputation," Burger went on, "for being

tricky, and I find that you *are* tricky, but I think they're legitimate tricks."

"I'm glad you think so," Mason told him. "Your predecessor in office didn't think so."

"I think an attorney has a right to work any legitimate trick in order to bring out the truth," Burger went on. "I notice that your tricks aren't for the purpose of confusing a witness, but for the purpose of blasting preconceived notions out of his head, so that he can tell the truth."

Mason bowed and said, "I'll thank you when you've entirely finished. Experience has taught me that words of praise like this are generally preliminary to a slap."

"No slaps this time," Burger went on. "I just want you to understand my attitude."

"If that's your attitude," Mason said, "I understand it."

"Then you'll appreciate what I'm going to say."

"Go on and say it."

"District attorneys have a habit of wanting to get convictions. That's natural. The police work up a case and dump it in the lap of the district attorney. It's up to him to get a conviction. In fact, the reputation of a district attorney is predicated on the percentage of convictions he gets on the number of cases tried."

Mason said in a very casual voice, "Go ahead, I'm listening."

"When I took this job," Burger said, "I wanted to be conscientious. I have a horror of prosecuting an innocent person. I have been impressed by your work. You probably won't agree with the conclusion I have reached concerning it."

"What's the conclusion?" Mason asked.

"That you're a better detective than you are a lawyer, and that isn't any disparagement of your legal ability, either. Your courtroom technique is clever, but it's all of it founded on having first reached a correct solution of the case. When you resort to unorthodox tricks as a part of your courtroom technique I'm opposed to them, but when you use those tricks to bring about a correct solution of a mystery I'm for them. My hands are tied. I can't resort to unorthodox, spectacular tactics. Sometimes I wish I could, particularly when I think a witness is lying to me about the identity of a criminal."

Mason said slowly, "Since you're being frank with me, which is something no other district attorney has ever done, I'll be frank with you, which, incidentally, is something I've never bothered to be with any other district attorney. I don't ask a man if he's guilty or innocent. When I start to represent him, I take his money and handle his case. Guilty or innocent, he's entitled to his day in court, *but* if I should find one of my clients was really guilty of murder and wasn't morally or legally justified, I'd make that client plead guilty and trust to the mercy of the Court."

Burger nodded his head heartily. "I had an idea you would, Mason."

"Remember what I said," Mason warned him, "that there was no moral *or* legal justification for the homicide. If a person is morally justified in killing, I'll save that person from the legal penalty if it's possible to do so."

"Well," Burger said, "I can't agree with you on that. I believe the law is the only machine of justification, but I want you to understand I'm not prejudiced against you and I would like to be friendly with you. Therefore, I want you to produce Hazel Fenwick."

"I don't know where she is."

"That may be true, and yet you may be able to produce her."

"I tell you I don't know where she is."

"You spirited her away."

"I sent her to my office."

"Your action in doing that is open to grave suspicion."

"I don't know just why," Mason said evenly. "If *you'd* been the first one on the scene you'd have thought nothing of sending her to *your* office so you could get a statement out of her."

"I'm a public official and it's my duty to investigate murder," Burger said.

"That doesn't prevent me from making an investigation on behalf of my client, does it?"

"It depends on how it's done."

"There's no secret of how it was done in this case," Mason told him. "I did what I did in the presence of witnesses."

"What happened after that?"

"Hazel Fenwick took my car and disappeared."

"I have reason to believe," Burger said, "that the woman's life is in danger."

"What makes you think so?"

"She is the only person who can positively identify the murderer."

"Not the murderer," Mason said. "The man who was seen coming out of the room."

"They're one and the same."

"You think so?"

"It stands to reason."

"Nothing stands to reason until it can be proven."

"Well, let us express it this way, then: It's a matter of opinion. You're entitled to yours and I'm entitled to mine. At least, the man *may* be the murderer. That man is desperate. I think that Hazel Fenwick either has met with foul play, or will meet with foul play."

"Therefore, what?"

"Therefore, I want to put her where she'll be safe."

"And you think I can tell you where she is?"

"I feel quite certain of it."

"I can't."

"Can't or won't?"

"Can't."

Burger got to his feet and said slowly, "I wanted you to understand my attitude. If your clients are innocent I want to know it, but, by God, if you think you can pull a stunt like the one you pulled in concealing that witness in a murder case and not get into trouble, you're crazy."

Mason said slowly, "I tell you I don't know where she is."

Burger jerked open the door to the corridor and paused in the doorway to deliver an ultimatum. "You've got forty-eight hours," he said, "to change your mind. That's final." The door shut.

Della Street glanced apprehensively at the lawyer.

"Chief," she said, "you've got to do something about that woman."

Mason nodded moodily, then grinned and said, "I can do a lot in forty-eight hours, Della."

11

PAUL DRAKE'S EYES SHOWED LOSS OF SLEEP.

"Whenever a detective gets to digging around in people's lives," he said, "he finds skeletons."

Mason nodded moodily and said, "Who is it this time, Paul?"

"Hazel Fenwick," the detective said.

The lawyer motioned to Della Street to make notes.

"What about her?" he asked. "Did you get anything out of those finger-prints?"

"I'll say I did," the detective said. "I got ten perfect finger-prints, pulled a few wires to get the dope I wanted, and found out all about her."

"Her prints are registered then?"

"I'll say they are. She's suspected of being a female Bluebeard."

"A what?"

"A female Bluebeard."

"All right, go ahead and spill it."

"The police haven't anything very definite," the detective said, "but this woman marries men, the men then die, and she inherits the property."

"How many men?" Mason asked.

"I can't find out. The police aren't sure, but they've got some pretty strong suspicions. One of her husbands had arsenic in his stomach. They started an investigation. They exhumed another husband and found more arsenic. They arrested her, took her finger-prints, questioned her, and didn't find out anything. While they were collecting more data, some kind-hearted friend slipped her a couple of saws. She sawed through the bars of the county jail, where she was being held, and disappeared."

Mason gave a low whistle, and said, "Any living husbands?"

"Yes. There's Stephen Chalmers. She married him and he walked out on her two days after the marriage. She didn't get a chance to feed him arsenic."

"Does he know about her past record?" Mason asked.

"No. I think he lied about his property when she married him. She found out the truth and there was quite a scene. Chalmers called her a gold digger and walked out. He hasn't seen her since."

"Are you sure of the identification?" the lawyer asked.

"Yes," Drake said. "I managed to copy the photograph from the back of Dick Basset's watch."

"I didn't know there was any photograph," Mason said.

"Neither do the police. Basset has the only photograph. He hasn't said a word about it."

"How did you get it?"

"Oh, I just figured he probably had one somewhere, so I picked his pocket, pried open the back of the watch, took a photograph of the photograph that was in it, and checked it with the police photographs on file in the Rogues' Gallery."

"And Chalmers identified the photograph?"

"Yeah, the one I'd stolen from Basset's watch. I didn't show him the police photographs because I didn't want him to know she had a record."

Mason said slowly, "Look here, Paul; do you suppose you could get Chalmers to let me get him a divorce if it didn't cost him anything?"

"Sure," Drake said. "But that might make him suspicious. He wants to get married again, anyway. Let him give you his note for a hundred bucks. He's a slicker and he'll beat you out of the note."

Mason nodded slowly and said, "All right, send him in. Tell him you can fix it up."

"But," the detective said, "what's the idea in getting the divorce?"

"I'm going to make a build-up," Mason told him.

"Build up to what?"

Mason said slowly, "The hardest thing on earth to describe is a woman. Notice the description of Hazel Fenwick which the police have given to the newspapers—height five feet two, weight one hundred and thirteen, age twenty-seven, complexion and eyes dark, last seen wearing a tailored brown suit with brown shoes and stockings."

"Well?" Drake asked.

"Darn few people ever saw this woman. She entered the picture mysteriously. Evidently Dick Basset courted her strictly on the quiet. The description is all anyone has to go by and that description would fit almost any dark-haired woman in the middle twenties."

Drake, watching him narrowly, said, "So what?"

Mason took Della Street's arm, piloted her to a corner, away from the detective, and said, in a whisper, "Go to an employment agency and find a young woman in the middle twenties, about five feet two, with dark hair and eyes, weight about one hundred thirteen, and who is hungry. If she's got a brown tailored suit, brown shoes and stockings, so much the better. If she hasn't, get her that kind of an outfit, and be damn sure she's hungry."

"How hungry?" Della Street asked.

"Hungry enough so she won't argue with cash."

"Will she go to jail?" Della Street inquired.

"She may, but she won't stay there, and she'll be paid for it if she does. Wait a few minutes before you go, Della. I've got a couple of other things."

He walked back to the detective and said, "Paul, you stand pretty well with the newspaper boys, don't you?"

"I think so. Why?"

"Slip one of your newspaper friends fifty bucks," the lawyer said. "Get him to take photographs of everyone in Basset's house. Tell him to say that he wants the pictures for his newspaper. Do you think you can do that?"

"Sure, it would be simple."

"All right, now here's the catch in it. I want those pictures taken at a particular place."

"What place?"

"I want the subjects sitting in the chair that Basset was sitting in when he was killed. I want close-ups that will show their facial expressions."

"Why that particular place?" the detective asked.

"That's a secret," Mason told him, grinning.

"It's pretty dark there."

"Not in the early morning," Mason said. "Have those pictures taken between nine and ten o'clock in the morning. Have the subjects facing that east window. Sunlight will be streaming in through that window."

The detective pulled out a notebook. "Okay," he said. "There's Overton, the chauffeur, Colemar, the Brite woman, Dick Basset, and who else?"

"Anyone else who had access to the house on the night of the murder."

"Seated at the desk?"

"Seated at the desk, facing the window."

"You want close-ups?"

"Yes."

"Okay," Drake said. "It sounds goofy, but I'll do it."

The telephone rang, Della Street picked up the receiver and said, "Hello," and passed it quickly across to Perry Mason, saying in an undertone, "It's Harry McLane on the wire. He wants to talk with you personally."

Mason waved Paul Drake through the door and said into the transmitter, "Yes, this is Mason talking."

Harry McLane's voice was high-pitched with excitement.

"Listen," he said. "I've been a damned fool. I was used as a cat's-paw and didn't realize it until just now. Now I know what a fool I've been. I'm going to tell you the whole business and make a clean breast of the entire affair."

"All right," Mason said, "come on in. I'll be waiting for you."

"I can't come," McLane said. "I don't dare to."

"Why not?"

"I'm being watched."

"Who's watching you?"

"That's part of the story I'll have to tell you when I see you."

"Well, when am I going to see you?" Mason asked.

"You'll have to come to me. I don't dare to try and come to your office. I tell you, I'm being watched, and it would be as much as my life was worth to see you. Now, listen. I'm registered at the Maryland Hotel under the name of George Purdey. I'm in Room 904. Don't ask for me at the desk. Come in the hotel, go up the elevator and walk down the corridor. If there's anyone in the corridor, don't hesitate as you walk by my room. Just keep right on going as though you were looking for some other room. If there's no one in the corridor, twist the knob of the door and step in. I'll leave it open for you. Don't knock."

"Listen," Mason said. "Tell me just one thing. Who was the accomplice? Who . . . ?"

"No," McLane said, "I won't tell you a damn thing over the telephone. I've told you too much now. If you want to come, come. If you don't, go to hell."

The receiver made noise at the other end of the line as it was slammed on the hook.

Perry Mason gently slipped the receiver back into position, glanced at Della Street and at Paul Drake.

"I've got to go out," he said.

"Can I reach you," his secretary asked, "if anything important should develop?"

Mason hesitated a moment, then scribbled on a sheet of paper the words, "Maryland Hotel, Room 904, care George Purdey." He folded the paper, put it in an envelope, sealed the envelope and handed it to her.

"If I don't call you within fifteen minutes," he said, "tear open that envelope. You, Paul, will then come for me at that address. And be certain to take a gun with you."

He reached for his hat and started for the door of the office.

12

PERRY MASON SLID HIS CAR IN CLOSE TO THE CURB A BLOCK and a half away from the Maryland Hotel. He sat at the steering wheel, smoking a cigarette, peering up and down the street for a matter of some fifteen or twenty seconds before he opened the door and got to the sidewalk.

He did not walk directly to the hotel, but swung around the block, and approached the hotel from a side entrance.

A clerk was on duty at the desk. Mason sauntered past him to the cigar counter, picked out a package of cigarettes, contemplated the cover of a magazine, drifted toward the elevators, and stepped into one of the cages just as the operator was on the point of closing the door.

"Eleventh floor," he said.

He got off at the eleventh, walked down two flights of steps to the ninth, and waited to make certain that the corridor was empty before he stepped from the stairway into the corridor. He strode purposefully to the door of 904, turned the knob without knocking, opened the door, stepped into the room, and pushed the door closed behind him.

The shades were down in the room. Drawers had been pulled from the dresser. A suitcase had been opened, and the contents were strewn over the floor. The body of a man lay face down on the bed, the left arm dangling down to the floor, the head lolling at an angle, the right arm doubled up under the chest.

Mason, taking care to touch nothing, tiptoed around the bed, dropped to his knees and leaned forward so that he could look up under the portion of the body which lay over the edge of the bed.

He saw that the man's right hand clutched the hilt of a knife; that the knife had been buried in the heart. The twisted features were those of Harry McLane.

Mason was warily watchful. He stepped back a couple of

paces and cocked his head to one side, listening. He fished in his left waistcoat pocket with thumb and fore-finger, pulled out one of the counterfeit eyes which Drake had had made. He polished the eye with his handkerchief so there would be no finger-prints on it, stepped to the side of the bed, bent forward and inserted the counterfeit eye between the loosely clutched fingers of McLane's left hand. He tiptoed to the door, polished the inner knob with his handkerchief, jerked open the door, stepped into the corridor, rubbed the outer knob hastily with his handkerchief, and let the door close behind him.

Mason walked swiftly to the stairs, climbed the two flights to the eleventh floor, rang for the elevator, and was whisked down to the lobby. He entered a telephone booth, called his office and said, "Okay, Della, burn that envelope."

He left the hotel, walked through an alley to the street where he had left his car, and stood concealed in the alleyway, looking up and down the street.

He spotted a police car, which was parked at the curb some fifty feet behind his own car. Two men sat in the police car, slouched down in the seat, as though they were prepared for a long wait.

They were watching Mason's car.

The lawyer narrowed his eyes in thoughtful scrutiny and stepped back into the alley. As he stood there, another car swung around the corner and slid to a stop directly opposite the police car. Sergeant Holcomb, of the Homicide Squad, leaped out from the driver's seat and conversed in low tones with the two men in the car.

Perry Mason abruptly turned and retraced his steps down the alley to the next street. He walked with quick steps to the hotel, entered the hotel, crossed to the clerk's desk, and said, "I'm not anxious to have the information broadcast, but I'm looking for a chap by the name of Harry McLane. I've got a tip that he's here in the hotel some place. Have you got a McLane registered?"

The clerk looked through the register, and shook his head.

"Funny," Mason said slowly. "I was told he'd be here. My name's Perry Mason. I'm going into the dining-room and get something to eat. If he should register, please have me paged. But don't tell him that I'm looking for him."

He stepped into the dining-room and ordered a sandwich and a bottle of beer. When the sandwich was brought to him, he accepted the check, and insisted on tipping the waitress a half-dollar. He ate the sandwich, leisurely, drank the bottle of beer, sauntered to the door of the dining-room and stood there looking into the lobby.

Sergeant Holcomb was standing in a corner of the lobby behind a potted palm.

Mason stepped back into the dining-room and walked directly to the public telephone near the cashier's desk. He dropped a nickel and asked for police headquarters.

"I want to speak to Sergeant Holcomb," he said.

"Sergeant Holcomb isn't in."

"Is there anyone who can take a message for him?"

"What about?"

"About some developments in connection with a case I'm working on."

"Who is this talking?"

"Perry Mason, the lawyer."

"What's the message?"

"Ask him to come to the Maryland Hotel as soon as he gets in. Tell him I'm waiting for him there."

He hung up the receiver.

He dropped another nickel and called the district attorney's office.

"Perry Mason, the lawyer," he said. "I want to talk to Hamilton Burger on a matter of considerable importance. . . . No, I won't talk with anyone else. I want to talk with Mr. Burger personally. Tell him Mr. Mason is on the line."

After a few seconds he heard Burger's voice, calm, suave, yet wary.

"What is it, Mason?"

"I'm down at the Maryland Hotel, Burger. I was told to come here by someone who gave me a tip over the telephone and wouldn't leave his name. I was told that Harry McLane was here, and was ready to talk. I've inquired at the desk, and McLane isn't registered here. I have an idea he may be coming in almost any minute. The voice of my informant sounded as though he knew what he was talking about.

"Now, McLane worked for Basset. It, incidentally, happens that he's a client of mine on another matter. . . ."

"Yes," Burger said, "I know all about that matter, Mason. You don't need to explain it."

"That simplifies things," Mason said. "You can appreciate the fact that McLane might give some important information if he wanted to."

" 'If he wanted to' is good," the district attorney said. "What do you want me to do?"

"I'm in rather a peculiar position in this thing," Mason explained. "In a way, I'm acting as attorney for McLane. Therefore, if he's going to talk, I'd like to have some representative of your office here when he talks. I've called Sergeant Holcomb at the Homicide Squad, but can't get him."

There was a moment of silence. Then Burger said, "You're at the Maryland Hotel now?"

"Yes."

"How long have you been there?"

"Oh, quite a little while. I waited around for McLane, and he didn't show up. I had a meal in the dining-room and put in a call for Sergeant Holcomb."

"Well," Burger said slowly. "I'll send a man down, if you think it isn't a wild-goose chase. But understand one thing—from the minute my man arrives, my office is going to be in charge."

"Okay by me," Mason said.

"Thank you for calling," Burger said, and hung up.

Mason slipped the receiver back into place, lit a cigarette, opened the door from the dining-room and walked into the lobby, taking care not to look in the direction of the corner where Sergeant Holcomb was standing, one foot on the rim of the tub which held the potted palm, his elbow resting on his bent knee, a cigarette between his fingers.

Mason walked to the desk and said, "McLane hasn't registered yet?"

"No."

Mason took a chair, sprawled out his legs, made himself comfortable and puffed placidly on his cigarette.

When the cigarette was three-quarters finished, he went to the desk again and said, "Say, I hate to keep bothering you, but this man McLane may have registered under another name. He's a young fellow about twenty-four or twenty-five, with celluloid-rimmed glasses. He has a few pimples on his face, dresses well, has light reddish hair, and freckles on the backs of his hands. I'm wondering if . . ."

The clerk said, "Just a minute. I'll get the house detective."

He pressed a button, and, a moment later, a paunchy man with hard, intolerant eyes stepped from an office and looked Mason over in uncordial appraisal.

"This is Mr. Muldoon, our house officer," the clerk said.

"I'm looking for a man whose real name is Harry McLane," Mason said, "but who may have registered under another name. He's about twenty-four or twenty-five, with a mottled complexion. He has light reddish hair and freckles on the backs of his hands. He's slender, well-dressed. The last time I saw him, he had on a dark blue suit, with a white stripe, and he wore a very light gray hat. I'm wondering if you'd remember him."

"What do you want him for?"

"I want to talk with him."

"But you don't know what name he's registered under?"

"No."

"How do you know he's here?"

"I was advised that he's here."

"Who advised you?"

"Really," Mason said, "I don't know as that's any of your business."

"You've got a crust," Muldoon told him, "coming in here and insinuating to me that one of our guests is a crook."

"I didn't insinuate any such thing."

"You insinuated he was registered under another name."

"A man might do that for lots of reasons."

"Well, suppose you come clean," the house detective said. "You're holding something back. Who are you? Why do you want . . . ?"

There was the sound of steps behind them. Muldoon looked up, stared for a moment with surprise, then let his lips break away from his teeth in a grin.

"Sergeant Holcomb!" he said. "I ain't seen you for a month of Sundays."

Perry Mason whirled with a quick start of feigned surprise. "I've been trying to call you," he said.

"From where?" asked Sergeant Holcomb.

"From here—from the hotel."

"What did you want with me?"

"I wanted to tell you about a tip that was given me, a tip that I think is hot."

"What was it?"

"That Harry McLane was at this hotel, and he wanted to talk."

"Well, have you seen him?"

"They say he isn't registered here."

"What's the excitement about with the house dick?"

"He described a guy," Muldoon said, "and wanted to find out if he was here in the hotel, registered under another name."

Sergeant Holcomb's eyes stared steadily at Muldoon.

"Is he?"

"Yes, I think so."

"What's the name?"

"George Purdey. He's in 904. He came in about an hour and a half ago. He looked phony, which is why I spotted him."

Sergeant Holcomb turned to Perry Mason.

"How long have you been here, Mason?"

"Quite a little while," Mason said.

"What have you been doing?"

"Been waiting for McLane to show up. I thought I'd got

here ahead of him. I was told he was going to register at this hotel, and that he'd be willing to talk."

"You said you were calling me?"

"Yes, I wanted to have some officer present when he talked —that is, if he was going to talk."

"What was he going to talk about?"

"Something about that Basset case. I don't know just what it was."

"Listen," Sergeant Holcomb said. "You can't fool me a damn bit. You didn't call me and you never intended to call me. You've been here over half an hour. What have you been doing?"

"I was in the dining-room."

"Getting something to eat, I suppose, because it just happened you were too hungry to wait."

Mason looked appealingly at the clerk.

"That's right, sir," the clerk said. "He said he was going into the dining-room."

"Where this bird says he's going, and where he goes, aren't always the same things," Sergeant Holcomb remarked. He took Mason's arm, and pushed him toward the dining-room.

"Come on, buddy," he said. "If you can pick out the girl that waited on you, I'm going to give you a written apology."

Mason stood in the doorway, looking uncertainly.

"I'm sorry," he said, "but I can't do it, Sergeant. You know I seldom pay attention to waitresses. I know it was a young woman in a blue uniform."

Sergeant Holcomb laughed sneeringly.

"They all have on blue uniforms," he said. "It's just like I thought, Mason. You can't get away with it."

"Wait a minute," the lawyer said. "That girl over there looks familiar."

Sergeant Holcomb beckoned to her with his finger.

"You wait on this man a few minutes ago?" he asked.

She shook her head.

Sergeant Holcomb sneered.

The waitress who had brought Mason his sandwich and beer came forward.

"*I'm* the one that waited on him," she said.

Mason's face suddenly lit with recognition.

"That's right," he said. "You are. I'm sorry but I didn't remember you very clearly. You see, I was rather preoccupied at the time."

"Well, I remember you all right," she said. "You gave me a fifty-cent tip for a sandwich and beer order. I don't get fifty-cent tips with sandwich and beer orders often enough to forget the people who gave them to me."

Sergeant Holcomb's face was a study in surprised consternation.

The cashier, who had overheard the conversation, said, "Why, I remember this gentleman. He paid his check and then stood at the telephone by the desk making a couple of calls."

"Who'd he call?" Holcomb asked.

"A Sergeant Holcomb at police headquarters, and then the district attorney's office. I thought he was a detective and I listened to the conversation."

"The district attorney's office!" Holcomb said.

"Why, yes," the cashier told him. "He called the district attorney when he couldn't get Sergeant Holcomb. He asked the district attorney to send a man over to be with him when he interviewed a chap by the name of McLane, who was a witness to something or other."

Sergeant Holcomb said slowly, "Well—I'll—be—damned!"

"What do we do now?" Mason inquired. "Do we talk with Harry McLane?"

"*I* talk with Harry McLane," Sergeant Holcomb said. "*You* wait in the corridor."

Holcomb pushed Mason toward the elevator.

"Ninth floor," he said.

They reached the ninth floor and Mason, hastily stepping from the elevator, started to walk in the wrong direction, then, glancing at the numbers on the rooms, caught himself, turned and walked down the corridor toward 904. Sergeant Holcomb caught Mason's sleeve and pulled him back.

"I'll be the one who makes the contact," he said. "You keep back of me."

He stood in front of the door of 904 and knocked gently. When there was no answer, he knocked again, then turned the knob of the door and opened it. He stepped inside the room and said over his shoulder to Perry Mason, "You wait there."

The door closed.

Mason stood motionless.

Abruptly the door opened. Sergeant Holcomb's white, excited face stared at Perry Mason.

"Is he going to talk?" the lawyer inquired.

"No," Sergeant Holcomb said grimly, "he's not going to talk. Now you're a busy man, Mason. Suppose you go right back to your law office. I'll attend to things here."

"But," Mason said, "I want to see McLane."

A spasm of impatience registered on Sergeant Holcomb's face.

"You," he said, "get the hell out of here before I get rough about it. This is one investigation I'm going to make before your masterly touch manipulates the evidence and spirits away the witness."

"Has something happened?" Mason asked, standing his ground.

"It will happen if you don't beat it," Sergeant Holcomb said.

Mason turned with dignity and said, "The next time I try to give you a tip you'll not know it."

Sergeant Holcomb said nothing but stepped back into the room and closed and locked the door.

Mason went directly to his car, drove to his office, pushed his way into Della Street's office and said, "Listen, Della, we've got to work fast. . . ."

He broke off as a figure stirred in the shadows. Pete Brunold, grinning, got up from his chair and extended a hand to Perry Mason.

"Congratulations," he said.

Sheer surprise held Mason motionless.

"You!" he remarked. "What the devil are you doing out of jail?"

"They turned me loose."

"Who did?"

"The cops—Sergeant Holcomb."

"When?"

"About an hour and a half ago. I thought you knew about it. You got a writ of *habeas corpus*. They didn't want to make a charge against me just yet, so they turned me loose."

"Where's Sylvia Basset?"

"I don't know. I think she's in the district attorney's office. They're questioning her."

Mason said slowly, "Probably the worst break you ever got in your life was when they turned you loose. You get out of here. Go to a hotel, register under your name, telephone the district attorney, and tell him that you're there."

"But why," Brunold asked, "should I telephone the district attorney? He doesn't . . ."

"Because I told you to," Mason interrupted savagely. "Damn it. Do what I tell you to. Seconds are precious—minutes might be fatal. Get started! I thought you were safely in jail, and any minute now . . ."

The door pushed open. Two men entered without knocking. One of them looked at Brunold and jerked his head significantly toward the door.

"Okay, buddy," he said. "Get started."

"Where?" Brunold asked.

"We're from the D.A.'s office," the man said. "The Chief wants to see you right now and it'll take more than a writ of *habeas corpus* to spring you this time. Your friend, Mrs. Basset, spilled some information to the D.A. We've got a warrant for you and she's already been arrested."

"What's the charge?" Mason asked.

"Murder," the man said grimly.

Mason said, "Brunold, don't answer any questions. Don't tell them . . ."

"Hooey!" one of the men said, grabbing Brunold's arm and pushing him toward the door. "He'll answer questions about where he spent his time during the last hour and a half or he'll have *two* murder charges against him."

"Two?" Brunold asked.

"Yeah," the man said. "Every time you get out of jail there's an epidemic of dead guys holding glass eyes in their hands. Come on, let's get started."

The door slammed shut behind them.

Della Street glanced inquiringly at Perry Mason.

Mason crossed the office in swift strides, jerked open the door of the safe, and took out the pasteboard box containing the bloodshot glass eyes. He crossed to the coat closet and took out an iron mortar and pestle. One by one, he dropped the glass eyes into the mortar and pounded them to fine dust.

"Della," he said, "see that I'm not disturbed."

13

PERRY MASON STUDIED THE DARK-HAIRED, DARK-EYED YOUNG woman who stared across the desk at him with something of defiance in her manner.

Standing to one side and slightly behind her, Della Street regarded Perry Mason anxiously. There was a superficial resemblance between the two women.

"Will she do?" asked Della Street.

Perry Mason's eyes surveyed the girl in silent appraisal.

"Your name?" he asked at length.

"Thelma Bevins."

"Age?"

"Twenty-seven."

"Training?"

"Secretarial."

"Been out of a job long?"

"Yes."

"Ready to do anything that's offered?"

"That depends on what it is."

Perry Mason remained silent.

She squared her shoulders, tilted her chin and said, "Yes, I don't give a damn what it is."

"That's better," Mason told her.

"Do I get the job?"

"I think you do, if you'll do exactly what I say. Can you follow instructions?"

"That depends on the instructions, but I can try."

"Can you keep quiet if you have to?"

"You mean not say anything?"

"Yes."

"I think I can."

"I want you," Perry Mason said, "to take an airplane to Reno. I want you to get an apartment in the name of Thelma Bevins."

"You mean, I'm to rent an apartment under my own name?" she asked.

"Yes."

"Then what do I do?"

"You stay there until a man comes to serve some papers on you."

"What sort of papers?"

"They'll be papers in a divorce action."

"Then what?"

"This man will ask you if your name is Hazel Basset, also known as Hazel Fenwick, formerly Hazel Chalmers."

"What do I do?"

"You say that your name is Thelma Bevins, but that you are expecting the papers and that you'll take them and accept service."

"Is there anything illegal in that?"

"Certainly not. They are papers which I will prepare and which you can expect. You know that they're going to be served on you because I'm telling you so now."

She nodded her head and said, "Is that all there is to it?"

"No," he told her, "that's the beginning."

"What's the ending?"

"You'll be taken into custody."

"You mean arrested?"

"Not exactly arrested, but you'll be taken into custody for questioning."

"Then what do I do?"

"Then is when the difficult part of it comes in. You keep your mouth shut."

"Don't tell them anything?"

"Don't tell them one single word."

"Shall I make any demands?"

"No, simply sit absolutely tight. You'll be questioned and cross-questioned. You'll be photographed by newspaper reporters. You'll be cajoled and wheedled. You'll be threatened, but you'll keep quiet. There's only one thing you will say, and you'll keep saying that."

"What is that?"

"That you refuse to leave the State of Nevada until some court of competent jurisdiction has given an order forcing you to cross the state line. Do you understand that?"

"I want to stay in Nevada, is that it?"

"Yes."

"What do I do to keep there?"

"Simply refuse to leave."

"Suppose they take me?"

"I don't think they'll take you. There's going to be a lot of publicity and a lot of newspaper reporters. If you insist on being allowed to remain in Nevada until some court has ordered your removal, they'll wait until they have a court order before they take you out."

"And that's all?"

"That's all there is to it."

"What do I get for it?"

"Five hundred bucks."

"When do I get it?"

"Two hundred now—three hundred when you've finished the job."

"How about expenses?"

"I furnish you an airplane ticket to Reno. You pay for your apartment out of the two hundred dollars."

"When do I start?"

"Right now."

She shook her head and said, "Not right now. When I get that two hundred dollars I go out and eat, *then* I start."

Mason nodded to Della Street.

"Give her two hundred dollars, Della," he said, "and have her sign a written statement that she is to go to Reno under my instructions; that she is to register under her own name; that when someone seeks to serve papers on her she will say her name is not Hazel Fenwick nor Hazel Basset nor Hazel Chalmers, but that she will accept the papers."

"What's the object of that?" Thelma Bevins asked.

"That protects you and it protects me," Perry Mason said. "It shows exactly what you're instructed to do. Above all, be sure that you don't lie. Don't say that your name is Hazel Fenwick. Don't say that your name is Hazel Basset. Never admit that you're anyone except Thelma Bevins. Simply say that you're expecting the papers and will accept service of them. Do you understand that?"

"I think I do," she said. "And I get three hundred dollars when it's over with?"

"That's right."

She leaned across the desk and gave Perry Mason her hand. "Thanks," she said. "I'll make a good job of it."

The telephone rang and Della Street, lifting the receiver and listening, glanced at Perry Mason.

"Paul Drake, Chief," she said.

Mason said, "Run Miss Bevins out through that side door, Della. I don't want Paul Drake to see her. She can go around and come in the office from the other entrance. Tell Drake to come in. I'll hold him here until you get finished with Miss Bevins. Then take her down to the plane and see her aboard. Just as soon as you hit Reno, Miss Bevins, get that apartment. You'll be there for less than a week, so rent it by the week. Wire me the address of the apartment. Don't sign the telegram. Do you understand?"

She nodded, and Della Street piloted her through the side door. A few moments later she appeared and ushered Paul Drake into the office.

"Thought I'd look in to see if things were coming all right," Drake said.

Mason nodded, and said, "They're okay, Paul."

"You contacted Stephen Chalmers all right?"

"Yes. I'm going to file his divorce action today."

"I got those pictures you wanted," Drake said. "I'll have the prints for you sometime tomorrow."

"Have any trouble?" Mason asked.

"Not a bit. We got everyone in the house, with one exception."

"Why the exception?"

"Colemar," the detective said. "He was last on the list and he smelled a rat. You see, Perry, I wanted to save you that fifty bucks. I didn't see any reason for having a newspaper photographer do the job. I got one of my men to pose as a reporter from the *Journal*. It got by okay until we came to Colemar. Seems that Colemar is going to be a witness. He'd just come from the D.A.'s office. He called them on the phone and asked if they wanted him to pose. Seems like they've warned him not to do or say anything unless he asks them. . . ."

"What did the D.A.'s office say?" Mason asked. "Did they smell a rat?"

"Evidently they did because Colemar hung up the telephone and then called the *Journal* and asked for the city editor's desk. That checkmated my man. He grabbed his camera and beat it. Can you get along without Colemar, Perry?"

"I think I can," Mason said, "if you're sure he's going to be a witness for the prosecution."

"Sure he is," the detective asserted. "He's been spilling something to them. They'd evidently told him not to do anything until he'd called them."

Mason nodded slowly and asked, "How about those other

pictures, Paul? Do they show anything peculiar about the facial expressions?"

"Nothing I can find," the detective said. "Look them over for yourself. Overton apparently tried to keep any expression whatever from showing on his face. Edith Brite had her lips compressed in a grim line. Dick Basset looks as though he were posing for a portrait, but the photographer told me he had a lot of trouble getting Dick to keep his eyes on the camera. Dick kept letting his gaze wander down to a spot on the floor. Does that mean anything?"

"It *may*," Mason said, "but probably it doesn't. I'll have to study the picture. How about this Brite woman . . . ?"

Drake interrupted him in a low voice, saying, "Listen, Perry, this may be serious as hell. You heard about young McLane?"

Mason nodded and said, "Yes, I heard some rumors. How do the police figure it, Paul? Was it murder or suicide?"

"I don't know. They're keeping it pretty close. But I'm wondering about that eye he was holding, Perry. You remember I got you a bunch of eyes. I'd feel a lot better if I saw that bunch of eyes again."

"Why?"

"I'd just like to make certain they're all there."

Mason shrugged his shoulders. "Those eyes, Paul, are all gone."

"Where?"

"Never mind where."

"Suppose they trace me through the wholesaler . . ."

"I told you," Mason interrupted, "not to leave a back trail."

"Sometimes a man can't help it."

"Then," the lawyer said, "it's just too bad."

"Look here, Perry. You said you'd keep me out of jail."

"You're not in yet, are you?"

The detective shivered and said, "I have a hunch I'm going to be."

Mason said slowly, "Paul, I think we'd better rush this case to trial. The district attorney wants to hold the preliminary examination day after tomorrow. I'm going to consent to it."

The detective puckered his forehead in a worried frown. "Look here, Perry, we're in this thing together. If . . ."

"Get your suitcase packed, Paul," the lawyer interrupted; "you're taking the next plane to Reno."

"To get away from this eye business?" Drake asked.

"No, to serve papers on Hazel Fenwick, sometimes known as Hazel Chalmers, also known as Hazel Basset."

Drake gave a low whistle and said, "So, you *did* know where she was!"

Mason lit a cigarette. "You make too damn many comments, Paul," he said.

Drake started for the door.

"I'm packing my suitcase, Perry, but just remember one thing—you promised to keep me out of jail."

Mason waved his hand in a gesture of dismissal and rang for Della Street. She entered the room just as the detective was leaving. Mason waited until the door closed, and then said, "Take a divorce complaint, Della. The ground will be desertion. The defendant will be described as Hazel Chalmers, also known as Hazel Fenwick, and sometimes known as Mrs. Richard Basset."

The secretary stared at him in open-mouthed surprise.

"Why," she said, "if you file the action that way, every newspaper in town will pounce on it. They follow the divorce actions as routine news."

Mason nodded. "I'm sending Paul Drake on to Reno by the evening plane," he said. "Get that girl started at once. When she wires us the address of her apartment, we'll wire Drake to serve papers on her there."

Della Street, watching him curiously, said, "A lot of the newspaper boys know that Paul Drake serves most of our papers."

Mason nodded his head slowly. "If," he said, "I can make the proper build-up on this thing, I can get away with it, but everything depends on the build-up. Go ahead and knock out that divorce complaint, then see that it gets filed."

14

JUDGE KENNETH D. WINTERS, THE JUDGE OF THE LOWER COURT, who was acting as a committing magistrate, fully appreciated the spotlight of publicity which had been focused upon him.

"This," he said, "is the time fixed for the preliminary hearing of Peter Brunold and Sylvia Basset, jointly charged with the murder of one Hartley Basset. Gentlemen, are you ready to proceed with the preliminary hearing?"

"Ready," said Perry Mason.

District Attorney Burger nodded.

Newspaper reporters squared themselves over their notebooks and settled down to business. The case was virtually unique, in that the district attorney himself was conducting a preliminary hearing, and every newspaper man in the room knew that there were events in the making.

"James Overton," said District Attorney Burger, "will you please come forward and be sworn."

Overton held up his right hand, stood staring over the courtroom, dark, saturnine, sardonic, yet, withal, with an air of polished poise about him which seemed, in some way, to set him apart from the others.

"Your name is James Overton and you were employed as a chauffeur for Hartley Basset?" Burger asked, as Overton, having been sworn, took the witness stand.

"Yes, sir."

"How long had you been employed by Mr. Basset?"

"Eighteen months."

"You were employed as chauffeur during all that time?"

"Yes, sir."

"What was your occupation before that time?"

Perry Mason pushed his way up from his counsel chair.

"I am aware," he said, "that it is usually poor policy for an attorney for the defense to enter a lot of technical objections at a preliminary examination. It is far better trial tactics to get the district attorney to expose his hand by asking everything that he wishes to. I am also aware that it is customary for a district attorney to put on only enough of a case to bind over the defendants, without giving to the defense any inkling of the case which he has built up. However, I sense there is perhaps something unusual in the present case. Therefore, I am going to ask the Court and Counsel whether any object can be served by going into this man's occupation prior to the time he entered the employ of Hartley Basset."

"I think it can," Burger said.

"Then I won't object," Mason announced smilingly.

"Answer the question," said Judge Winters.

"I was a detective."

"A private detective?" Burger inquired.

"No, sir, I was employed by the United States Government in connection with some of its intelligence work. I left the government and took employment with the municipal police department on the detective bureau. I had been working only a few days when Mr. Basset approached me and asked me to accept employment as his chauffeur."

Perry Mason settled back in his chair. His eyes drifted over to Brunold's face, then to Sylvia Basset.

Brunold, flanked by a deputy, sat with an expressionless face. Sylvia Basset's eyes were wide with surprise.

"During the time you were employed as chauffeur for Hartley Basset, did you have any duties other than driving an automobile?" Burger asked.

"We'll stipulate," Perry Mason said, with a sneer in his voice, "that this man was employed to spy upon the wife of Hartley Basset and that he endeavored to ingratiate himself with his master by reporting facts which made such espionage seem necessary."

Burger was on his feet.

"Your Honor," he thundered, "I object to such tactics on the part of the defense. He is seeking to discredit the testimony of this witness by a slurring offer to stipulate something which can't be stipulated to."

"Why not?" Perry Mason asked.

"Because it isn't a fact," said Burger. "This man is a reputable investigator, and . . ."

"They're all the same," Mason interrupted.

Judge Winters banged his gavel. "Gentlemen," he said, "I am going to have no more such discussions. And you, Mr. Mason, will make no more interpolations. You will confine your remarks to the Court and the cross-examination of witnesses, subject to your right to make objections in a proper and respectful manner."

Perry Mason nodded, sprawled out in his chair and smiled slightly.

"Your Honor," he said, "I beg the Court's pardon."

"Go on, Mr. Burger," said Judge Winters.

Burger took a deep breath, seemed to control his temper with an effort and said, "Just answer the question, Mr. Overton. What other duties did you have?"

"I was employed by Mr. Basset to keep him advised as to certain things that went on in his household."

"What things?"

"He told me that he wanted me to be his listening post."

"Was 'listening post' the expression he used?"

"Yes."

"Now, then, let me first lay the preliminary foundation. When did you last see Hartley Basset?"

"On the fourteenth."

"Was he alive?"

"He was when I first saw him on that date."

"The last time you saw him, was he alive?"

"No, sir, he was dead."

"Where was he?"

"He was lying in his inner office, sprawled out on the floor, a blanket and a quilt, folded together, lying near one side of his head, his arms outstretched, a .38 Colt Police Positive revolver lying on the floor near his left hand, a .38 caliber Smith and Wesson revolver near his right hand. This second gun was concealed under the blanket and quilt."

"And Mr. Basset was dead?"

"Yes, sir."

"You know that of your own knowledge?"

"Yes, sir."

"Who was present in the room at the time you saw Mr. Basset's body?"

"Sergeant Holcomb of the Homicide Squad, two detectives whose names I don't know, and a criminologist who works with the Homicide Squad. I think his name is Shearer."

"Did you notice anything in the left hand of the corpse?"

"Yes, sir."

"What was it?"

"A glass eye."

"Was that glass eye marked at that time and in your presence by any of these gentlemen, so that it could be identified again?"

"Yes, sir."

"By whom was it marked?"

"Mr. Shearer."

"What mark was placed upon it?"

"He took some black substance—ink, or a nitrate of silver compound—I don't know just what it was, and made certain marks on the interior surface of the eye."

"Would you recognize that eye if you saw it again?"

"Yes, sir."

Burger produced a sealed envelope, went through an elaborate formality of cutting open the envelope, shook out a glass eye, and handed it to Overton.

"Is this the eye?"

"Yes, sir, that's it."

"Had you ever seen that eye before?" Burger asked.

Overton nodded his head emphatically.

"Yes, sir," he said, "I had seen that eye before."

"Where?"

"In the possession of Mr. Basset."

Perry Mason sat forward in his chair, his eyes slitted in thoughtful concentration.

Burger glanced at him triumphantly. "You mean," he said, "that you saw this eye in the possession of Mr. Basset *before* the murder?"

"Yes, sir."

"How long before?"

"Twenty-four hours before."

"Was that," asked Burger, spacing the words so as to get the utmost dramatic effect from the question, "the first time you had ever seen that bloodshot glass eye?"

"No, sir," said Overton.

Judge Winters did the witness the honor of leaning forward and cupping his hand back of his ear, so that he might miss no word.

Burger asked impressively, "When did you first see that eye?"

"About one hour before I first saw it in Basset's possession."

"Where was it then?"

"Just a moment," Perry Mason said. "I object to the question on the ground that it is incompetent, irrelevant, immaterial, assumes a fact not in evidence, and no proper foundation has been laid."

"Specifically, what does your objection relate to, Counselor?" Judge Winters asked.

"To the fact that it is a conclusion of the witness as to whether the eye which he saw in the hand of the dead man is the same eye that he saw twenty-four hours before or twenty-five hours before, depending upon which occasion he is now about to testify to. Your Honor will remember that there was an identification mark placed upon the eye *when it was taken from the hand of the dead man.* The witness is able to testify now and identify the bloodshot eye by reason of that identifying mark.

"But, your Honor, prior to the time that identifying mark was on the eye, all that the witness knows is that he saw *a* bloodshot glass eye, rather than *the* identical bloodshot glass eye concerning which the question has been asked."

Burger chuckled.

"Very well," he said, "we will concede that the objection is well taken upon the ground that no proper foundation has been laid, and with the permission of Court and Counsel, we will withdraw that last question and proceed to lay the proper foundation.

"Did you see a similar glass eye—that is, one which was similar in appearance to the one which was found in the hand of the dead man?"

"Yes, sir."

"When?"

"I first discovered it about twenty-five hours prior to the murder. I handed it to Mr. Basset and saw it in his possession about twenty-four hours prior to the murder."

"Have you any way of telling whether that was the same eye as the one which you have now identified and which you are holding in your hand?"

"Yes, sir."

"You have a way of making such identification?"

"Yes, sir."

"What is it?"

"At the time I discovered this eye, I was wearing a diamond ring. I knew from my experience as a detective the importance of identifying . . ."

"Never mind what you knew from your experience as a detective," Burger said. "That may go out by stipulation and consent. Just tell what you did."

"I took my diamond ring and cut a cross on the inner surface of the eye."

"Is that cross readily visible?"

"No, sir, not unless you look at it in just the right light. I didn't cut it deeply enough to be conspicuous."

"Can you tell whether that cross now appears upon the eye which you hold in your hand?"

"Yes, sir, it does."

"We ask," Burger said, "that the eye be received in evidence as the People's Exhibit A."

"No objection," Mason said.

"It will be so received," Judge Winters announced.

"Then that is the same eye which you saw some twenty-five hours before the murder?" Burger went on.

"Yes, sir."

"Where did you find it?"

Overton took a deep breath, then said in a voice which filled the courtroom, "In Mrs. Basset's bedroom."

"How did you happen to find it there? Under what circumstances?"

"I heard a noise in Mrs. Basset's bedroom."

"What kind of a noise?"

"The noise of conversation."

"You mean you heard voices?"

"Yes, sir, and motions."

"And what did you do?"

"I knocked on the door."

"What happened?"

"There was the sound of hurried motion."

"Was the conversation that you heard," Burger asked, "distinguishable?"

"You mean as to words?" the witness asked.

"Yes."

"No, sir, it was not. I could hear the rumble of a man's voice and the sound of a woman's voice, but I couldn't hear the words."

"What happened after you knocked on the door?"

"There was this period of excited motion. Then I heard a window open and close. Then I heard Mrs. Basset's voice saying, 'Who is it?' "

"And what did you say?"

"I said, 'Open the door, please. This is James, the chauffeur.' "

"Then what happened?"

"There was an appreciable interval. Then she said, 'You'll have to wait until I get dressed.' "

"Then what happened?"

"Then I waited for perhaps a minute."

"And then what?"

"Then she unlocked the door and opened it."

"What did you do or say?"

"I said, 'I beg your pardon, Madam, but Mr. Basset thought

there was a burglar in the house. He wanted me to make certain that the windows were all fastened.' "

"What did she say?"

"Nothing."

"Did you say anything further?"

"Yes, sir, I told her that I was sorry if I had disturbed her, that I didn't think she had retired."

"What did she say then, if anything?"

"She said that she hadn't retired; that she had been taking a bath."

"Then what did you do?"

"I crossed the room to the window."

"Was the window open or closed?"

"Open."

"It is on the second story?"

"Yes, sir, but there is a roof some six feet below the window and a trellis leading to the roof."

"Did you see any signs on the window sill of an unusual character?"

"I saw this glass eye."

"Where was it?"

"On the floor."

"Had Mrs. Basset seen it?"

"Objected to as calling for a conclusion of the witness," Mason said. Then, as he saw Judge Winters hesitating, said, "Oh, well, I'll withdraw the objection. Let's hear his story."

"No, sir," Overton said, "she hadn't seen it."

"What did you do?"

"I stooped and picked it up."

"Did she see what you had picked up?"

"No, sir, she had her back turned to me at the moment."

"And what did you do then?"

"I slipped the eye in my pocket."

"Then what?"

"Then I left the room and, as soon as I had left the room, she closed and locked the door behind me. Then I scratched the cross on the inside of the eye with the diamond on my ring, and went at once to Mr. Basset."

"Then what happened?"

"Mr. Basset tried to identify the eye. He asked me to get in touch with some reputable manufacturer of artificial eyes, and see if there was any way in which the eye could be identified."

"Did you do so?"

"I did so."

"We will," said Burger, "let the identification of the eye speak for itself. In other words, we will not ask this witness to qualify as an expert. We will place upon the stand the expert whom he consulted and let him identify the eye."

He turned to Perry Mason and said, "You may cross-examine."

"You are certain that it was a man's voice that you heard?" Mason asked, "referring to the time that you heard the conversation through the keyhole of Mrs. Basset's room?"

"I didn't say it was through the keyhole," the witness snapped.

Mason's smile was urbane.

"But it *was* through the keyhole, was it not, Mr. Secret Service Man?"

A titter ran through the courtroom. Judge Winters pounded with his gavel.

"Go on," Mason said, "answer the question. Was it or was it not through the keyhole?"

"I heard it through the keyhole, yes," Overton said.

"Exactly," Mason remarked. "Now, what did you *see* through the keyhole?"

"I couldn't see anything. That is, nothing that was of any value."

"Could you see Mrs. Basset moving around in the room?"

"I saw someone."

"Do you think it was Mrs. Basset?"

"I'm not certain."

"But you didn't *see* any man?"

"No, sir."

Perry Mason elevated his arm and stretched a long, accusing forefinger at the witness.

"Now," he said, "when Mr. Basset was killed, his murderer escaped in the Basset automobile, did he not?"

"No, sir."

"You're certain about that?"

"Yes, sir."

"Why are you so certain?"

"Because, shortly after the body was discovered I heard that a witness had said the murderer had escaped in the Basset automobile. So I went at once to the garage to ascertain if the car was missing."

"Was it missing?"

"No."

"Did you feel the radiator to see if it was warm, or look at the temperature indicator?"

"No, I didn't do that. But the car was there just as I had left it, in the place that it should have occupied."

Mason smiled, waved his hand, and said, "That is all."

"Just a minute," Burger said. "One question on re-direct examination. You have testified that you couldn't see the man who was in that room."

"That's right."

"Could you hear him?"

"I could hear his voice, yes."

"You're certain that it wasn't a radio that you heard?"

"Yes."

"Was it Richard Basset that you heard?"

"No, sir."

"How do you know?"

"Because I know Richard Basset's voice. And, while I couldn't distinguish words, I could distinguish the tone of the voice."

"Did you," asked Burger, "notice any peculiarity about the man's speech?"

"Yes, sir."

"What was it?"

"He talked in a quick, excited manner, talking very, very rapidly. That is, the words came out so fast that they all seemed to run together."

"That is all," Burger said.

"Just one question," Mason interpolated. "You couldn't hear the words?"

"No, sir."

"Then how did you know the words all ran together?"

"Just from the way the man was talking."

"But you couldn't tell when he had finished one word and started on another? In other words, you couldn't distinguish the words?"

"I think I could."

"You *think* you could?"

"Well, I'm not certain."

"We'll let it go at that," Mason said, smiling.

Burger waved Overton from the stand.

"Call Dalton C. Bates," he said.

A tall, quick-stepping individual came nervously forward, held up his right hand, was sworn, and took the stand.

"Your name?" Burger asked.

"Dalton C. Bates."

"Your profession?"

"I'm a maker of artificial eyes."

"How long have you been making artificial eyes?"

"Ever since I was fifteen years of age. I started an apprenticeship in Germany at that age."

"Is there any particular advantage in studying in Germany?"

"Yes, sir."

"What is it?"

"All of the glass that is used in making artificial eyes is manufactured in two places in Germany. The formula under which the glass is manufactured is kept secret. It has never been duplicated in this country. It takes a certain particular type of glass."

"Where did you study in Germany?"

"I served an apprenticeship in Wiesbaden."

"Over what period of time?"

"Five years."

"Then what did you do?"

"Then I worked with one of the best artificial eye experts in Germany for ten years. I came to San Francisco and studied for a while with Sidney O. Noles. Then I started in business for myself, and since that time I have been manufacturing artificial eyes."

Perry Mason sat forward on the edge of his chair, his eyes surveying the witness.

"You're qualifying this man as an expert?" he asked of the district attorney.

"Yes," Burger said shortly.

"Go ahead, then," Mason said.

"The making of artificial eyes is a profession, and a highly specialized profession?" Burger asked.

"Yes, sir. Very much so."

"Can you describe how an artificial eye is made—that is, generally?"

"Yes, sir. The glass is first blown into a ball. That is, the glass comes in a tube. It is then blown and pinched off in the flame in such a manner that it forms a ball. The particular color of glass chosen is that which will match the white of the eye to be duplicated.

"The iris of the eye is then built up on the surface of the ball by the use of solid bits of colored glass which are blended carefully while the glass ball is being rotated. If you will study the human eye you will see that it is composed of numerous colors. While one color predominates, there are various different shades in the iris. These shades must not only be duplicated, but the glass must be fused in such a manner that there is not only a true color, but a true formation of the little color patches, and of brilliance, as well. The pupil is made by using a very black glass which, incidentally, is backed with purple, and the size and shape of the pupil must be carefully considered.

"It is also necessary to study the blood supply of the eye which is to be duplicated. Veins must be traced upon the artificial eye. These veins are more plentiful on either side of the iris, and vary greatly in color with the individual, some having a yellowish tinge, some being redder than others, some being more prominent.

"When the eye is finished, it is covered with a clear crystal, which is fused onto the glass. After this is done, the ball of glass is cut by a torch and molded into shape.

"I have given you only a brief outline of the steps involved."

Burger nodded and said, "It is, then, a very specialized profession?"

"Very much so."

"Can you give us any better idea of what a specialized profession it is?" Burger asked.

"I can tell you this," Bates said. "There are not more than thirteen men in the United States who are recognized as being first-class artificial eye makers. There are so many things which enter into the making of an eye; first, there must be a very expert manipulation of the materials; then there must be a certain individual artistry of color blending. A really successful maker of artificial eyes must combine the skill of an artist, when it comes to blending colors, with the craftsmanship of a very expert glass-blower."

"It is, therefore, possible to recognize the work of certain individuals," Burger asked, "in the same manner that an artist could recognize the work of another artist by reason of the manner in which the pigments were applied?"

"In many instances it is," Bates said.

"I will," Burger said, "hand you herewith an artificial eye, which has been introduced in evidence as People's Exhibit A. It is an eye which was found clasped in the hand of a murdered man. I will ask you to examine such eye and state whether or not you can tell anything concerning that eye."

Bates looked at the eye which Burger handed him and nodded his head.

"Yes," he said, "I can tell a great deal about it."

"What can you tell?" Burger asked.

Judge Winters frowned, looked at Perry Mason as though expecting an objection. When he heard none, he said to Burger, "The question is rather peculiarly put, Counselor."

"There is no objection," Mason said.

"This eye," Bates stated, "was made by a very expert crafts-man. I think that I can give the name of that craftsman. He is one who resides in San Francisco. The eye is a bloodshot eye. That is, it is an eye which was made to be worn only on occasions, yet, the eye has been worn, or used, as you may care to put it. The man who wore it is one who has a very high degree of bodily acidity."

"How," asked Burger, "can you tell that?"

"By this ring, which you can see about the edge of the eye. That is caused by body acids entering the glass and causing a slight discoloration. After a certain period of use, this dis-coloration becomes quite pronounced. It can be partially re-moved by a bleaching treatment, but the life of the eye is shortened by these body acids which enter the glass and which cause it to become unduly brittle."

Burger nodded to Perry Mason.

"With your permission, Counselor," he said, "I will ask this witness questions concerning another eye, which I will sub-sequently identify. In order that there may be no question of taking advantage of Counsel, I will state that the eye, con-cerning which I am about to interrogate Doctor Bates, was one which was found in the hand of another dead person, to wit, one Harry McLane."

"It is your contention," Judge Winters asked, "that you have the right to introduce evidence of more than one crime, Counselor?"

"No," said Burger, "I am introducing evidence only against these defendants for the murder of Hartley Basset. The evi-dence which I am now about to introduce is evidence to ex-plain motivation."

"Very well," Judge Winters said, "it will be limited to that purpose."

Burger opened another envelope, took from it an artificial eye, and dropped it into the extended palm of the witness.

"What can you tell us about this eye, Doctor?"

"This eye was not as carefully constructed as the other. It is, I would say, a stock eye. That is, it is an eye which was not made to order for any particular person, but is one of a large stock of eyes such as is kept by any well-equipped optician in a large city."

"What are your reasons for making that statement, Doctor?"

"The eye was completed and was covered with crystal. It was then a clear eye—that is, it was an eye made to match a normally clear eye. After it was covered with crystal, a hurried attempt was made to simulate a bloodshot eye. These little glass veins, which give the white of the eye the bloodshot appearance, were put on after the crystal covering had been placed on the eye. There is no trace whatever of any color line on the eye, and I would, therefore, say that it had not been worn, at any rate, for any appreciable period of time, particularly by the person who wore the other eye which you first gave me."

"May we," Burger asked, "have this eye marked, for identification, as People's Exhibit B?"

"No objection," Mason said.

"Let it be marked for identification," Judge Winters ordered.

"Cross-examine," Burger said.

Mason asked casually, "Why should a person have a so-called bloodshot eye, Doctor?"

"Some people are very sensitive about their artificial eyes. They don't want it known that they have them. For that reason, they go to elaborate precautions to keep from being discovered. They have eyes made to wear in the evening; eyes to wear when they're not feeling well; eyes made to wear when their natural eye is inflamed."

"In other words, then, it is difficult to tell when a person has an artificial eye?"

"Very difficult."

"Why is it necessary to have a separate eye to wear in the evening?"

"Because the size of the pupil of a natural eye varies during the day. With the glare of bright light, the pupil contracts. At night, under artificial lights, the pupil is larger."

"Is it, then, virtually impossible to detect the wearer of a well-made artificial eye?"

"If the socket is in proper shape and the eye is properly fitted, yes."

"The wearer of such an eye has the ability to move the artificial eye?"

"Oh, yes."

"How is the artificial eye held in the socket?"

"By a vacuum. The eye is fitted in in such a manner that the air between the artificial eye and the socket is virtually all removed."

"It should, then, be a difficult matter to remove such an eye."

"It is not difficult, but the lid must be pulled down in a manner to let air in back of the eye before it can be readily removed."

"That is done by the wearer of the eye?"

"Yes. The lid must be pulled down."

"Quite far down, Doctor?"

"Quite far down."

"Then," Perry Mason said, "if a man with a well-fitted artificial eye was committing a murder and bending over the man he was murdering, it would be an impossibility for his artificial eye to drop out accidentally, would it not?" There was a gasp of surprise from the crowded courtroom, as the spectators realized the point which Mason had been driving home.

"Yes," Doctor Bates said, "it would be virtually impossible."

"So that, if a murderer, emerging from a place where he had committed a murder, exhibited an empty eye socket, it would be because he had, himself, deliberately removed the artificial eye which was in that socket. Isn't that a fact, Doctor?"

"I would say so—yes. That is, of course, conceding that the murderer wore an eye which was properly fitted."

"Such an eye as that which was first given you by the district attorney, and which was claimed to have been found in the hand of Mr. Hartley Bassett?"

"Yes."

"That eye, in your opinion, was carefully fitted?"

"Yes, sir. That eye was made by an expert."

Mason waved his hand.

"That is all, Doctor," he said. "Thank you."

Burger leaned forward in frowning attention. His eyes were puckered into a worried look.

"Your next witness," said Judge Winters.

"Mr. Jackson Selbey."

A well-tailored individual, wearing a very high, starched collar, shuffled importantly forward, held up a well-manicured right hand, took the oath, walked to the witness chair, carefully hitched up his trousers, so as to preserve the crease, crossed his knees, and smiled at Burger, after the manner of one who is accustomed to discharging his duties with dapper efficiency.

"Your name?" Burger asked.

"Jackson Selbey."

"What is your occupation, Mr. Selbey?"

"I am manager of the Downtown Optical Company."

"How long have you been employed as manager for that company?"

"Four years."

"Prior to that time where did you work?"

"For the same company, but in the position of chief clerk. I was promoted to the position of manager at the time I mentioned."

"The Downtown Optical Company keeps a stock of artificial eyes, does it, Mr. Selbey?"

"Yes, sir; a very complete stock."

"Are these eyes as well or as carefully made as eyes which are made by the more expert artisans, such as Doctor Bates mentioned in his testimony?"

"They are quite well made. They are made in various color combinations, so that any normal eye may be readily matched. They are well enough made to make a very satisfactory match for any natural eye."

"Do you, in your stock, carry a supply of what might be called bloodshot eyes—that is, eyes in which the veins over the white part of the eye are sufficiently red and pronounced to give the eye a bloodshot appearance?"

"No, sir."

"Why not?"

"Because such eyes are required only by persons who go to great lengths to prevent the detection of artificial eyes. Such persons usually employ one of the recognized experts to match their natural eyes, whereas the person who purchases artificial eyes from us does so because he wishes to save money. He usually doesn't have sufficient funds to have a complete set of eyes."

"Have you, however," Burger asked, "upon occasion, been asked to make bloodshot eyes?"

"Yes, sir, upon one occasion."

"And how was it suggested that be done?"

"By taking an eye from stock and having an eye maker add bloodshot veins to it by using the very fine reddish vein-glass which is manufactured for such purpose."

"Was that recently?"

"Yes, sir."

"I will ask you," Burger said, "to look at the people present in this courtroom and tell us if you have seen any of these persons in your store."

"Yes, sir, I have."

"Did one of them order the bloodshot eye to which you have referred?"

"Yes, sir."

"Who was that person?"

Selbey pointed his finger at Brunold.

"The defendant, Brunold, sitting there," he said, "was the man."

The eyes of the court attachés and spectators turned toward Brunold. Brunold sat, arms folded across his chest, chin slightly sunk forward, eyes fixed. His face was absolutely without expression.

It was Sylvia Basset whose face showed the emotion which newspaper reporters like to describe in sensational articles. She bit her lip, leaned forward to stare at the witness, then sat back with an audible, tremulous sigh.

"When did he order the bloodshot eye?" Burger asked.

"At nine o'clock in the morning, on the fourteenth of this month."

"What time does the Downtown Optical Company open its doors?"

"Nine o'clock in the morning."

"He was there when the doors opened?"

"Yes, sir."

"What did he say, if anything?"

"He said that it was necessary for him to have a bloodshot eye at once. He said he wanted an eye to take the place of the one which he had lost."

"Did he say when the eye had been lost?"

"Yes, sir, the night before."

"Did he mention a time?"

"No, sir."

"Did Mr. Brunold tell you under what circumstances the eye had been lost?"

"Yes. I told him we couldn't possibly make the eye he wanted, as he wanted it and within the time limit he had fixed. So he then gave me a story by way of explanation and, apparently, in an attempt to enlist my sympathies."

"Who was present at the time of this conversation?"

"Just Mr. Brunold and myself."

"Where did the conversation take place?"

"In the consulting room of the Downtown Optical Company."

"What did Mr. Brunold say?"

"He said that he had been calling upon a former sweetheart who had since married a man who was very jealous; that on the previous evening he had been talking with this woman when one of the servants had knocked on the door. Mr. Brunold said he had wanted to face the husband and have it out with him, but that the woman, because her son had been legally adopted by the husband, had refused to leave. He said that the woman pretended to have been bathing so that she could delay the servant's entrance long enough to enable Brunold to jump out of a window and make his escape. He further said that the bloodshot eye, which he customarily carried with him in a chamois-lined pocket in his waistcoat, had dropped from his pocket when he climbed from the window; that he was afraid the husband had recovered the eye and would trace it; that if this was done the husband would uncover a lot of information which would be damaging to the woman, and work a great injustice upon her.

"He then said it was necessary for him to have an eye to take the place of the one he had lost at once, so that he could either claim he had never lost the eye, or, if it appeared more to his advantage to do so, he could claim that someone had stolen his eye and substituted a counterfeit, and that he was afraid the person who had stolen the eye intended to 'plant' it where it would get him into trouble."

"And you're certain," Burger asked, "that the man who made these statements to you was none other than the defendant, Peter Brunold, who is now sitting here in court?"

"Yes, sir."

Burger smiled triumphantly at Perry Mason.

"Now, Counselor," he said, "you may cross-examine."

Perry Mason nodded, got to his feet, pounded his heels belligerently across the courtroom to the counsel table where the district attorney sat.

"Please let me have that second eye," he said, "which was marked, for identification, People's Exhibit B."

Burger handed him the eye in the stamped envelope, saying, as he did so, "Please be *very* careful to return the eye to that marked envelope, Counselor."

Perry Mason said, "Certainly. I am no more anxious than you are to get these eyes confused, although, with the expert testimony you have produced, we should be able to identify them in the event such a confusion takes place."

He advanced to the witness, shook the eye out of the envelope, and said, "Calling your attention to an eye which has been marked, for identification, People's Exhibit B, I will ask you whether *this* was the counterfeit eye which you sold to Peter Brunold."

Selbey shook his head, and his lips twisted in a triumphant smile.

"No, sir," he said sweetly, "it was not."

"It was not?" Mason demanded triumphantly.

"No, sir. You see, *we* didn't sell Mr. Brunold any eye. He appeared and said that he *wanted* such an eye, and explained the reasons why he wanted it. But we refused to make the eye. Doubtless he was able to get some other firm to do so."

15

PAUL DRAKE CAME CROWDING THROUGH THE SPECTATORS AS the courtroom buzzed with the activity of a recess. He paused just before the mahogany railing in the courtroom, waited until he had caught Perry Mason's eye, then gave him a significant wink.

Mason moved over to a corner where there was some opportunity for privacy. Paul Drake joined him.

"Well," the detective said, "I ranked the job. Have you seen the newspapers?"

"No," Mason said. "What happened?"

Drake opened a brief case, took out a newspaper still damp from the press, handed it to Perry Mason with a wry face, and said, "That tells the story—not as well as I could tell it, but it's a damn sight easier for me if you read it rather than have me tell it."

Mason didn't look at the newspaper immediately. He folded it under his arm and stared steadily at the detective.

"How'd you get back?" he asked.

"I chartered the fastest plane I could get in Reno and came back here in nothing flat. I think we averaged two hundred miles an hour or something like that."

"Even so," Mason told him, "the telegraph wires are quicker. How does it happen they're just getting out this news?"

"The smart boys in Reno tried to sew it up," Drake told him. "At least, that was the plan they were working on when I left. They wanted a complete confession and weren't going to release the news until they'd got it."

"Did they get it?"

"I don't know."

"Now then," Mason said, "who was going to confess to what?"

"Hazel Fenwick," Drake said, avoiding the lawyer's eyes.

One of the deputies entered the courtroom with half a dozen newspapers under his arm. He rushed over to the district attorney, handed him one, and Burger, frowning irritably, snapped open a paper and started reading.

Mason moved over toward a corner as the deputy vanished in the direction of the Judge's chambers.

"How bad did you rank it, Paul?" he asked.

"Plenty," the detective told him.

"Well, go ahead and tell me about it."

"I'd rather you'd read about it."

"Hell!" Mason exclaimed impatiently. "I can read about the stuff they're handing the public, but what I want to know is how it happened that you slipped up on the job."

"I don't know."

"Well, go ahead and tell me the whole thing and perhaps I'll know when you get done."

"I followed your instructions," Drake said slowly, his eyes remaining downcast, "and took a plane to Reno. I arrived there, went to the telegraph office, called for telegrams, and found the message for me from Della Street telling me where to go to make the service. I stuck the telegram in my coat pocket, went up to a hotel, got a room, took off my coat and washed up. A bell boy came in to ask me if I had all the towels I wanted, and all that sort of stuff—that is, Perry, I thought at the time he was a bell boy."

"Go on," Mason said ominously. "Then what?"

"So far as I knew at the time, nothing," Drake told him, "but afterwards, when I looked through my coat pockets for that telegram, I couldn't find it. But that wasn't until quite a bit later."

"Go on," the lawyer said impatiently, "let's have it."

"Honest to God, Perry, I'd covered my back trail just as well as I could. I didn't figure I was tailed on the plane."

"Plane was crowded?" Mason asked.

"Yes, to capacity."

"Anyone try to talk with you?"

"Yes, a couple of men had a bottle and they tried to get me started. When they didn't click, a baby doll came over. Looking back at it, I can see there was something fishy about it, but right at the time I figured it was a case of a girl making her first trip by plane and being a little frightened."

"What did she do?"

"She sort of smiled at me," Drake said, "and when she was walking past my chair the plane gave a little lurch and she took a fall into my lap. . . . Oh, hell, you know how those things happen."

"Did you talk?" Mason asked.

"Not much on the plane. You can't hear well enough. But I bought her a drink at Sacramento."

"Did you talk then?"

"A little."

"Tell her who you were?"

"I gave her my name."

"Tell her what you were doing?"

"No."

"Didn't tell her your occupation?"

"No."

"Didn't give her a card?"

"No."

"Give her any information at all?"

"Not enough to put in your eye."

"What were you talking about?"

"I don't know, Perry. I was just handing her a line. I'll swear there wasn't anything more to it than that—you know the type of stuff you dish out to a frail who seems to be falling. I pretended I thought she was a motion picture star flying over to Reno for a divorce, kept trying to place her, swore I'd seen her on the screen some place, and knew she was one of the famous actresses, but told her I didn't go to the movies much, so I couldn't be sure which one."

"She seem to fall for that line?" Mason asked.

"She ate it up."

"She was a plant," the lawyer said.

Drake exclaimed, with the irritation of a man who has lost much self-respect and some sleep, "Of course she was a plant. What the hell! Do you think I'm dumb enough so I don't know she was a plant? But I didn't know it at the time. You wanted to know what happened and I'm telling you."

"Okay, go ahead and tell me what happened then."

"After I'd taken a wash and a drink in the hotel," Drake said, "I went down and caught a cab. I gave the cab driver the address of the apartment house."

"You didn't look at the telegram then?"

"No, I'd read it before and I remembered the address. It was easy to remember."

"Go ahead."

"I found the joint was an apartment house. I gave the apartment a ring and she buzzed the door open without asking any questions over the speaking tube. I took an elevator and went up. It was one of those wheezy automatic elevators. You know the type."

"Yes, I know," Mason said impatiently. "Go on and tell me what happened."

"I walked down the corridor to her apartment. The corridor wasn't very well lighted. I had to use a flashlight to pick up the number easily. I tapped on the door. She opened it.

"I didn't pull the papers out of my pocket right then. I kept my voice low and turned loose the best grin I could get, as though I was some guy who had been told by her sister to look her up."

"What did you say?" Mason asked.

"I asked her if she was Hazel Fenwick. She gave me a dead pan and said, 'No.'

"I looked a little bit surprised, and asked her if she wasn't Hazel Basset.

"Her face took on just a bit of expression. She said no, she wasn't Hazel Basset, but she didn't make any move to close the door. I was sizing her up pretty closely, and she tallied okay with the description I had of the Fenwick woman, so I decided it was time to put her on the defensive. I held her with my eyes, whipped the papers out of my pocket and told her that I was there to make service of some papers on Hazel Fenwick or Hazel Basset.

"She said very slowly, as though she'd been memorizing it, 'My name is Thelma Bevins, *but* if you have papers to serve on Hazel Fenwick or Hazel Basset I'll accept service of the papers.'

"Well, you know how it is in this game. You don't ask too many questions. I figured that was all the break I needed. I handed her the papers and she took them. About that time, I heard someone moving at my side. The door of an adjoining apartment on the other side opened in a hurry. I took a swift look and saw the place was filling up with men. I didn't get the sketch, but I knew damn well no one was going to keep me from serving those papers, so I pushed them into her hands, and about that time flashlights started to go off. I thought I was the center of a circus.

"Of course I knew then what had happened, but by that time it was too late. Just to make sure, I reached for the telegram. It wasn't in my coat, but I'll say one thing: Those birds had worked fast. They'd used this fake bell boy to frisk my coat while I was washing. They'd evidently known I was coming and what I was coming for. They were laying for me. Why, damn it, one of the smart boys was even parked on the fire escape right out from the girl's window! He stuck a camera through the window and busted the glass in order to do it. He took a flashlight just as I handed her the papers."

"Newspaper men?" Mason asked.

"Newspaper men and cops. Don't make any mistake about that town, Perry. The newspaper boys stand right in with the cops—at least, they do when it's an outsider who is getting the rooking."

"What did the cops do?"

"One of them," Drake said, "took a swing at my jaw. I got pretty much out of his way, but his fist was big as the business end of a pile driver and part of it took off a little skin. The others grabbed the girl and started strong-arming her down the corridor."

"How about the papers?" Mason asked.

"Oh, it's a service all right," Drake told him, "as far as that's concerned. They rushed her down the corridor but she was still holding the papers in her right hand. I'd shoved them into her hand when I saw the place start to fill up and she'd taken them mechanically and was still hanging onto them. I think she was the most surprised woman in the world."

"Do you know what happened next?"

"Sure, I know what happened. I heard them start giving her a brow-beating third degree all the way down the corridor. They were trying to find out who had paid her expenses to Reno, why she'd gone there, who had told her to come there, and all of that stuff."

"What did she say?"

"Nothing. She said she wasn't going to talk until she saw her lawyer."

"Then what?"

Drake said, "I knew the beans were spilled all over everything as far as Reno was concerned. I figured that they'd probably try to keep her covered up until after they'd got a confession. I knew you were in the middle of this trial and I didn't want them to hang a surprise on you out of a clear sky, so I went down to the airport, hunted up the bird who had the fastest plane in the country and paid him to burn a streak through the sky."

"Did he do it?"

"I'll say he did it," Drake said fervently.

Perry Mason frowned thoughtfully, slowly opened the newspaper, and read headlines:

MYSTERY WITNESS FOUND IN RENO

ADMISSIONS IMPLICATE LOCAL ATTORNEY

DISTRICT ATTORNEY'S OFFICE SAYS ENTIRE MATTER WILL GO BEFORE GRAND JURY

Mason slowly folded the paper.

"God, I'm sorry, Perry," Paul Drake said.

"Why, in particular?" Mason asked.

"Because it's put you in a sweet spot. You know as well as I do that jane will crack under the strain, if she hasn't already. She'll tell them the whole story. From what I read in the newspaper, it looks as though she's coughed up everything."

"Tell me," Mason said, "does she insist on staying in Nevada?"

"I don't know," Drake answered slowly, "just what she did at the time, but before that bunch of cops got done with her, she was ready to do anything or say anything, or I'm a cock-eyed liar."

Mason said slowly, "Watch out. Here's the D.A. coming over this way."

Burger surveyed Perry Mason with a frosty smile, and said, with the manner of one who is playing with a victim as a cat plays with a mouse, "If you have no objection, Counselor, I would like to have this hearing adjourned sometime today in order to go before the Grand Jury with a very important matter."

"Could you," asked Perry Mason, "have one of your deputies handle the matter before the Grand Jury so we could go on with this hearing?"

"Not very well," Burger told him. "And I can assure you, Counselor, it won't make the slightest difference to you."

"Why not?" Mason asked.

"Because," Burger told him, "you'll also be before the Grand Jury. It's in relation to the sudden trip to Reno of a certain Hazel Fenwick."

"Oh," Mason said, "am I to understand that Hazel Fenwick is here?"

"She will be."

"And she was in Reno?"

Burger said, with some show of feeling, "You know damn well she was in Reno. She's told the officers that you paid her expenses there. She's admitted that much. So far, that's as far as she will go. She claims her name is Thelma Bevins. That's the alias she was registered under in Reno. That's what she's told the boys in Reno. They didn't have the dope on her. She'll sing a different tune when I get her here and have her identified."

There was the bustle of activity. Judge Winters emerged from behind a black-curtained doorway and stepped to the bench. A gavel pounded the spectators to attentive silence.

Judge Winters looked down at Perry Mason. His facial expression was stern. He didn't say in so many words that he had read the newspapers, but the tone of his voice spoke volumes as he looked directly at Perry Mason and said, "Do you wish to proceed, Counselor?"

Perry Mason returned his gaze steadily.

"Yes, your Honor," he said.

16

JUDGE WINTERS NODDED TO THE DISTRICT ATTORNEY.

"Proceed," he said.

District Attorney Burger turned to one of the deputy sheriffs and nodded his head.

The man approached Perry Mason, a folded paper extended.

"Your Honor," the district attorney said, "there have been some rather startling, although not entirely unexpected, developments in connection with this case, and in connection with another matter which, while not directly involved, is nevertheless related to it. In view of this other matter, it will be necessary for me to ask for a brief adjournment of this hearing within approximately an hour."

Judge Winters frowned.

Burger went on, "I feel that I am violating no confidence, your Honor, in stating that this matter is one which is being investigated by the Grand Jury and it will be necessary for me to appear before the Grand Jury."

"Has the defense," asked Judge Winters, "any objections?"

Before Mason could say anything, Burger, raising his voice, said, "The defense *can* have no objection, because one of the first witnesses who will be called by the Grand Jury is none other than Perry Mason, the attorney for the defendants."

Mason said in slow, level tones, "Your Honor, that remark was uncalled for and unnecessary. I hold in my hand a subpoena to appear before the Grand Jury, a subpoena which very apparently was held in the hands of a deputy sheriff and could have been served at any time prior to the convening of court. Yet that paper was served at a signal from the district attorney, and purely for the purpose of letting the Court and the spectators know publicly that I was being called as a witness before the Grand Jury. It was merely a grandstand play."

Judge Winters hesitated a moment, and Burger, turning belligerently to Perry Mason, said, "I see you can dish it out, but you can't take it."

Judge Winters banged his gavel.

"That will do, Mr. District Attorney," he said. "There will be no further personal remarks of that nature, and I can assure Counsel for the defense that the Court will not allow its decision to be influenced in the slightest by the comments of Counsel. Proceed with the case, gentlemen."

Perry Mason, holding the subpœna in his hand, turned to scan the faces of those in the courtroom. He caught the anxious, startled eyes of Della Street on the outskirts of the crowd. She raised a newspaper in her hand and gestured with it significantly.

Perry Mason nodded his head almost imperceptibly and then flashed her a swift wink.

"Your next witness," Judge Winters said to the district attorney.

"George Purley," Burger announced.

As Purley was taking the oath, Burger turned to Mason and said, "Purley's reputation as a handwriting expert should be too well known to require formal qualification. He has been with the police department for years and . . ."

"I'll stipulate Mr. Purley's qualifications, subject to the right to cross-examine," Mason said.

Burger nodded perfunctory thanks and turned to the witness.

"Your name is George Purley, and you are now and for some time past have been employed as a fingerprint and handwriting expert with the police department?"

"Yes, sir."

"On the fourteenth of this month did you have occasion to go to the house of Hartley Basset?"

"I did."

"I will ask you generally if you noticed the body of the man who lay on the floor of the office in the Basset residence."

"I did."

"Did you notice a portable typewriter on the table near that body?"

"I did; yes, sir."

"Did you notice a piece of paper on which typewriting appeared, and which was in the typewriter?"

"Yes, sir."

"I show you this piece of paper and ask you whether that is the same piece of paper."

"It is."

"Did you make tests to determine whether the typewriting

on this paper was written by the machine in which the paper was found?"

"I did."

"What did those tests show?"

"They established conclusively that the typewriting was not done by that machine, but was, in fact, done by another machine that we subsequently found in the house."

"Where?"

"In the bedroom of Mrs. Basset, one of the defendants in this case."

"Did she make any statements in your presence as to the ownership of that machine?"

"Yes, sir."

"What did she say?"

"She said that it was her machine and that she used it for her private correspondence; that occasionally she typed her correspondence personally and occasionally had one of her husband's stenographic assistants type the correspondence."

"Did she mention anything about her qualifications as a typist?"

"Yes, sir; she said she had been a professional typist for years and used the touch system."

"What is meant by a touch system?"

"A system of typing in which the operator does not look at the keys of the typewriter, but strikes entirely by a sense of touch."

"Is there anything about this typing by which you can tell whether the person operating the machine used a touch system?"

"Yes, sir; a certain evenness of touch by which all of the keys were struck with approximately the same force. In the so-called two-finger system or hunt-and-peck system, because the pressure is less mechanical, the keys are struck with varying force and there is a very slight difference in the impression made by the type upon the paper."

"In your opinion, Mr. Purley, this paper was written upon a machine other than the one in which it was found and by a person using the touch system. Is that right?"

"Yes, sir; beyond any possibility of doubt this document was typed upon the Remington Portable which was found in Mrs. Basset's bedroom. In my opinion it was typed by a person who used the touch system and who was, or at least had been at some time, a professional typist."

"Cross-examine," Burger said briefly.

"If I understand the testimony correctly," Mason said, "this paper was typed upon the machine which was subsequently found in Mrs. Basset's bedroom. After it was typed, it was taken to the room where the body was found, and inserted in the typewriter. Is that correct?"

"Yes, sir."

"Thank you," Mason said. "That is all."

Judge Winters made a note in his notebook, nodded his head to Burger and said, "Your next witness, Counselor."

"Arthur Colemar," Burger announced.

Colemar came forward, took the oath, and slid into the witness chair, his gray eyes blinking as though he were slightly bewildered at his surroundings.

"Your name's Arthur Colemar?"

"Yes."

"What's your occupation, and by whom were you last employed?"

"I was Mr. Hartley Basset's secretary, sir."

"How long had you been employed by him?"

"For three years."

"When did you last see him?"

"On the fourteenth of this month."

"Was he living or dead?"

"Dead."

"Where was he?"

"In his inner office."

"How does it happen that you saw him there then?"

"I had been to a show. I returned to find the house in confusion. People were running about, apparently very much excited. I inquired the cause of the trouble, and was informed that Mr. Basset was dead. Someone took me into his office so that I could identify him."

"I think," Burger said, "that I have already proven the *corpus delicti,* so I won't go into the matter of death by this witness at any greater length. I desire to show by this witness certain other facts."

Judge Winters nodded. Mason, sitting sprawled in his chair, his legs thrust out in front of him, said nothing.

"You are, of course, intimately acquainted with the defendant, Mrs. Sylvia Basset."

"Oh, yes, sir."

"Mr. Basset has his office in his house?"

"In the same building, yes, sir. It had originally been designed, I believe, as a duplex dwelling, or as a four flat building, I don't know which."

"And Mr. Basset had the east side of the building for his office?"

"The lower floor on the east side, yes, sir."

"Where did you sleep?"

"I slept upstairs in the back part of the house."

"Where did you work?"

"In the part Mr. Basset had set aside for his office."

"Did you have occasion, from time to time, to talk with Mrs. Basset?"

"Frequently."

"Did you ever have an occasion to converse with her concerning the amount of life insurance Mr. Basset was carrying?"

"Yes, sir."

"When was that conversation?"

"Objected to as incompetent, irrelevant, and immaterial," Mason said.

"Overruled," snapped Judge Winters, his countenance cold as granite.

"Your Honor," Burger said, "I intend to prove motive by this witness. I feel that I am within my rights, and . . ."

"The objection has been overruled," Judge Winters said. "Moreover, this Court will never sustain an objection that such a question is not material. Experience shows that the motive of gain is one of the most compelling motives in murder cases. If the prosecution can establish this as a motive, it is undoubtedly entitled to do so."

Mason shrugged his shoulders and settled down in his chair.

"This conversation," the witness said, "took place about three days before Mr. Basset's death."

"Who was present?"

"Just Mrs. Basset, Richard Basset and myself."

"*Where* did the conversation take place?"

"In the hallway at the head of the stairs near the entrance to her bedroom."

"What was said?"

"She asked me if I was familiar with Mr. Basset's business affairs, and I told her I was. She asked me precisely how much life insurance Mr. Basset was carrying. I told her that I would prefer she take that up with Mr. Basset. She told me not to be foolish, that the insurance was carried for her protection, and she said, as nearly as I can remember, 'Colemar, you know that I'm the beneficiary in the insurance.'

"I didn't say anything, and after a moment she said, 'I am, am I not?' And then I said, 'Of course, Mrs. Basset, since you put it that way, there's no reason why I should contradict you. But I would prefer you talked over the nature, extent and type of the insurance with Mr. Basset.'

"She said she thought Mr. Basset was carrying too much insurance, and that she was going to ask him to drop some of the policies."

"Did she say precisely which policies?"

"No, sir."

"Then the effect of her conversation was to reassure her mind upon the fact that Basset was carrying . . ."

"Objected to as argumentative and calling for a conclusion of the witness," Perry Mason said. "This man is now testifying as to the motive of the defendant's question. The words speak for themselves."

"Sustained," Judge Winters said.

"Now, then," Burger went on, his face showing dogged determination, "are you acquainted with Mr. Peter Brunold, one of the defendants in this case?"

"I am, yes, sir."

"When did you first become acquainted with him?"

"About a week or ten days ago."

"How did it happen?"

"He was just leaving the door of the house as I drove up. He said that he had been looking for Mr. Basset but Mr. Basset was out, and he asked me if I knew when Mr. Basset would be back."

"What did you tell him?"

"I told him Mr. Basset would not be back until late."

"And Brunold was coming *out* of the house at that time?"

"Yes, sir."

"Where had you been?"

"Attending to some errands for Mr. Basset."

"You were driving Mr. Basset's car?"

"Yes, sir, that's right—the big sedan."

"That was the first time you saw Mr. Brunold?"

"Yes, sir."

"Did you see him again at a later date?"

"Yes, sir."

"When?"

"The night of the murder."

"And when did you see him then?"

"I saw him running away from the house."

"You mean the Basset house?"

"Yes, sir."

"Let's not have any misunderstanding about that. When you say the house, you mean the house where Mr. Basset had his office, and where he resided?"

"That's right. Yes, sir."

"And you say Mr. Brunold was running away from that house?"

"That's right."

"At what time was this?"

"Just as I was returning from the show I mentioned."

"How were you returning?"

"I was walking."

"Did you speak to Mr. Brunold?"

"No, sir, I didn't. Mr. Brunold didn't see me. He ran on past me on the other side of the street."

"Could you see him plainly?"

"Not all of the time, but when he passed under a street light, I was able to get a good look at his features. I saw him then and recognized him."

"Then what happened?"

"Then I approached the house and saw that something unusual was taking place. I saw figures running back and forth past the windows. They were moving rapidly."

"What did you see, if anything?"

"I saw Mrs. Basset and her son, Richard Basset."

"What were they doing?"

"They were bending over someone in the reception room. Then Mrs. Basset ran and called Edith Brite. I saw Edith Brite come running from the other part of the house and enter the reception room."

"What did you do?"

"I went to the reception room and asked what was the matter and if there was anything I could do. I could see someone was lying on the couch. I thought it might be Mr. Basset. I asked if he'd been hurt. Mrs. Basset came and stood in front of me and pushed me out of the door. She told me to go to my room and stay there."

"What did you do?"

"Followed instructions and went to my room."

Burger said to Mason, "Cross-examine."

Mason, arising from his chair at the counsel table, said, "Later on you went to the study and identified Hartley Basset's body, didn't you?"

"Yes, sir."

"At that time, did you hear it said that the young woman who had been lying on the couch when you first entered the house on your return from the picture show would know the man she had seen leaving the study if she saw him again?"

"Yes, sir, I heard there was such a witness."

"She was in a darkened room, but the light was streaming over her shoulder so that, while her own features were in the shadow, the light illuminated the features of this man after she had torn the mask from his face."

"I heard that was the case, yes."

"What's the object of this?" Burger asked. "Are you trying to get a lot of hearsay evidence into the record? We object to anything Hazel Fenwick may have said."

"It is," Mason pointed out, "part of the *res gestae*. I have a right to test this witness's recollection upon what happened immediately after he entered the house."

"But," Burger pointed out, "only for the purpose of testing his recollection, and not for the purpose of establishing what happened."

"That's all I'm asking him so far."

"Very well," Burger said. "With the understanding that your examination is limited for that purpose, I will make no objection."

Mason turned to Colemar.

"Now," he said, "if a man were wearing a mask, it would be because he wished to conceal the distinctive portions of his face, wouldn't it?"

"That question, Counselor," said Judge Winters, "is argumentative."

"I am not going to object," Burger said. "I am going to give Counsel a free hand."

"Thank you," Perry Mason said. "The questions are preliminary. I merely wanted to point out one or two things to the witness in order to prepare a preliminary foundation for some of the questions I intend to ask later."

"Go ahead, Counselor," Judge Winters said, "in view of the fact that the prosecution is making no objection."

"Did it impress you as improbable," Mason asked, "that a man, using a mask to cover the distinctive portions of his countenance, would exhibit an empty eye socket through that mask, thereby disclosing the *most* distinctive portion of his features, to wit, the fact that one eye was missing?"

"I'm sure I don't know, sir," Colemar said.

"I'm merely asking you," Mason said, "if that portion of Miss Fenwick's story did not impress you at the time as being unreasonable."

"I don't think so. No, sir."

"Now, obviously," Perry Mason went on, "the fatal shot was fired from a gun which was concealed under a blanket and a quilt, thereby muffling the sound. Isn't that correct?"

"That was what I gathered from my inspection of the premises, sir."

"It is perfectly obvious," Mason said, "that a masked man could not have entered Mr. Basset's study carrying a blanket and a quilt folded over his arm, and got close enough to his victim to have fired a shot, without having alarmed Mr. Basset. Isn't that true?"

"I would suppose so."

"Yet, from the position in which Mr. Basset's body was found, it appeared that he had been sitting at his desk and had simply slumped forward when the shot was fired. He had made no struggle, had not pulled the gun which was in a shoulder holster. Isn't that correct?"

"Your Honor," Burger interrupted, "these questions are plainly argumentative and speculative. This witness is not an expert and . . ."

Perry Mason smiled urbanely.

"I think," he said, "that Counsel is entirely correct."

A commotion took place in the back of the courtroom. Men swirled about into little, grunting eddies of human flotsam. Perry Mason raised his voice so that he held the attention of the Court.

"Your Honor will understand," he said, "that this witness has definitely placed *both* of the defendants in compromising positions. I feel, therefore, that I am entitled to examine him as to his motives, and . . ."

The disturbance in the back of the courtroom grew in volume. A man's voice said, "We're officers. Make way!"

Judge Winters pounded his gavel and looked at the back of the courtroom, his facial expression showing judicial irritation vying with human curiosity.

Burger jumped to his feet.

Perry Mason, already on his feet, gave Burger no chance to be heard. He raised his own voice and shouted, "Your Honor, I demand that I shall have the undivided attention of this witness and of the Court. If for any reason this is impossible, I demand that this witness be withdrawn from the stand until I have an opportunity to examine him without having the attention of both the witness and the Court distracted."

Burger said smoothly, "If the Court please, I was going to suggest that same thing. An unavoidable interruption is taking place. I was going to suggest the witness be withdrawn. . . ."

Judge Winters banged with his gavel repeatedly.

"Order!" he shouted. "Or I'll clear the courtroom."

"I'm an officer," a man from the back of the courtroom said.

"I don't care who you are," Judge Winters shouted. "You'll be fined for contempt of court. Court is in session."

"May it please the Court," Burger insisted with courtesy, but with his voice showing a very definite firmness, "I am perfectly willing for this witness to be withdrawn. In fact, I shall ask that he be withdrawn. A most important witness is entering the courtroom. I desire to examine this witness, and when I have examined her, I think I will not need to call any more witnesses. Except, *perhaps*, as to Mrs. Basset's complicity in the crime. I think this witness will definitely clinch the case of the prosecution against Brunold."

"And I object to that statement as improper, as argumentative, and assign it as misconduct," Mason shouted.

Burger, his face coloring, exclaimed, "Just throwing up a smoke screen in order to divert attention from yourself. You'll have plenty to worry about in a moment . . ."

"Order!" Judge Winters interrupted. "I'll have order in this courtroom, and I'll have no more personalities between Counsel. Be quiet or I'll clear the courtroom!"

A measure of silence descended upon the court. Burger, his face flushed, said in a choking voice, "Your Honor, I forgot myself. I beg the Court's pardon. . . ."

"Your apology is not accepted," Judge Winters said sternly.

"This Court has cautioned you before about engaging in personalities with Counsel. Now, what is it you wish?"

Burger controlled himself with a visible effort. His voice was strained and tense.

"I wish to withdraw Mr. Colemar from the stand in order to place this other witness on the stand. I would, however, like to have a few moments' recess."

"If," Mason said, "Counsel wants to put this witness on the stand, he should be willing to do it without interrogating her first and in private."

"Your Honor," Burger protested, "this is a hostile witness. She has absented herself from the jurisdiction of the court. I will have to handle her as a hostile witness. But her information is of the greatest value."

"You are referring to Hazel Fenwick?" asked Judge Winters.

"Yes, your Honor."

Judge Winters nodded his head.

"You, Mr. Colemar, may leave the stand. Let Miss Fenwick come forward."

"Those men will have to make way, your Honor. The aisles are crowded," Burger pointed out.

"Clear the aisles!"

"If we might have a few moments' recess," Burger pleaded.

Judge Winters hesitated a moment, then said, "The court will take a five minute recess."

Two officers came pushing their way down the aisle, a woman held between them, her face white.

Judge Winters, rising from behind the bench, stared curiously at her for a moment, then strode through the black-curtained doorway into his chambers.

Every eye in the courtroom turned toward the slender, well-formed, dark-haired young woman.

She flashed one pleading, anguished glance at Perry Mason, then swiftly averted her eyes. The officers pushed her forward. Someone held open the gate in the mahogany rail, and she entered the space reserved for the lawyers.

Burger approached her with an ingratiating smile. Spectators in the courtroom craned their necks eagerly forward, trying to see what took place. Those who could not see tried to listen. There was none of that buzzing hum of excited conversation which usually characterizes the recesses taken during an important murder trial. There was only the slight rustling motion which came from bodies leaning forward and the sound of people breathing.

Burger looked about him appraisingly, then took Thelma Bevins by the arm, piloted her to a corner of the courtroom near the court reporter's desk, and started whispering to her.

She shook her head doggedly. Burger glowered at her, shot forth a barrage of whispered comments, then apparently asked her some question. She half looked at Perry Mason, but caught herself before she had completely swung her head toward the attorney, looked back at Burger and clamped her lips shut.

Burger's hoarse threat was audible to those sitting in the front row of the courtroom chairs.

"By God," he said, "if you try that stunt, I'll put you on the witness stand under oath and *make* you talk. This is a preliminary examination. Whatever you have to say in connection with it will be material. I'll prosecute you for perjury if you lie, and the Judge will jail you for contempt of court if you don't talk."

Her lips remained closed.

Burger's face took a darker shade. He glared across the courtroom at Perry Mason, who, urbanely nonchalant, was lighting a cigarette.

Burger took a watch from his pocket and said, in that same hoarse voice, "I'm giving you one more chance. You have just sixty seconds to talk, and talk straight."

He stood staring at his watch. Thelma Bevins, standing very straight, stared past him, her eyes fixed disdainfully upon distance, her face very white, her lips clamped together.

An enterprising newspaper reporter, taking advantage of the fact that court was not in session, focused his camera, raised a flashlight bulb, and shot a picture—a picture which showed Thelma Bevins, grim and defiant, Burger holding his watch, belligerent and impatient, while, in the background,

Perry Mason, watching them with an expression of sardonic humor on his face, was puffing a cigarette.

Burger whirled on the reporter and shouted, "You can't do that!"

"Court ain't in session," the reporter said, turning and pushing his way through the crowd with his prized picture.

Burger snapped his watch in his pocket.

"Very well," he told Thelma Bevins, "you've made your bed. Now you can lie in it."

She gave no sign that she had heard him, but stood staring, as rigid as though she had been carved from marble.

Judge Winters reëntered the courtroom from his chambers, ascended to his seat on the raised dais, and said, "Court will reconvene. Are you gentlemen ready to resume the trial?"

Perry Mason drawled, "*Quite* ready, your Honor."

Burger's face showed rage. He said, "Hazel Fenwick, take the stand."

The woman did not move.

"You heard me!" Burger shouted. "You're to take the stand. Hold up your right hand and be sworn, and then sit on that chair."

"My name is not Hazel Fenwick."

"What is your name?"

"Thelma Bevins."

"All right, then, Thelma Bevins. Hold up your right hand to be sworn, and then take the witness stand."

She hesitated for a moment, then held up her right hand. The clerk administered the oath. She stepped to the witness chair and sat down.

"What's your name?" Burger said, in a loud tone of voice.

"Thelma Bevins."

"Did you ever go under the name of Hazel Fenwick?"

She hesitated.

Perry Mason's voice was suave and somewhat patronizing. "Now, Miss Bevins," he said, "if you don't want to answer that question, you don't have to."

Burger whirled to him and said, "Are you now appearing as this young woman's attorney?"

"Since you ask it, yes."

"That," Burger said, "puts you in a very questionable position, particularly in view of the question which has arisen as to your connection with her absenting herself from the state."

Mason bowed and said, "Thank you, Counselor. I'm quite capable of estimating the consequences of my own acts. I repeat, Miss Bevins, you don't need to answer that question."

"But she *does* need to answer it," Burger said, facing back toward the witness and pointing his finger at her. "You *have* to answer that question. It's a pertinent question, and I demand an answer."

Judge Winters nodded and said, "It happens, Counselor Mason, that it rests with the Court to say what questions shall be answered and what shall not be answered. This is a pertinent question, and I order the young woman to answer it. In the event she does not, I will be forced to hold her in contempt of court."

Perry Mason smiled reassuringly at Thelma Bevins.

"You don't need to answer it," he said.

Judge Winters gave an exclamation. Burger whirled to face Perry Mason, with his exasperation showing on his countenance.

Perry Mason went on in the same tone of voice, as though he had merely paused in the middle of a sentence, ". . . if you feel that answering the question would tend to incriminate you. All you need to do, Miss Bevins, is to say, 'I refuse to answer upon the ground of my constitutional privilege that the answer might incriminate me.' When you have once said that, no power on earth can make you answer the question."

Thelma Bevins flashed him a smile and said, "I refuse to answer the question upon the ground of my constitutional privilege that the answer might incriminate me."

A deadlocked silence fell upon the group clustered about the witness chair. At length, Burger sighed. The sigh was an eloquent acknowledgment of defeat.

He turned once more toward Thelma Bevins.

"You," he said, "were in the Basset residence at the time when Hartley Basset was murdered, weren't you?"

She glanced at Perry Mason.

"Refuse to answer the question," Mason said.

"How can an answer to such a question incriminate her?" Burger asked of Judge Winters.

Mason shrugged his shoulders and said, "I think, if I understand my law correctly, that is for the witness to decide for herself. It may be that an explanation might be more incriminating than an answer."

Thelma Bevins, taking her cue from Perry Mason's remarks, smiled. "At any rate, I refuse to answer the question, which *should* settle the point."

Judge Winters cleared his throat, but said nothing. Burger frowned, then plunged savagely into another line of attack.

"You know Perry Mason?" he asked.

Judge Winters, leaning forward, said with judicial solemnity, "There certainly is nothing in an answer to that question, either one way or the other, which could be incriminating. The Court, therefore, directs you to answer the question."

"Yes," she said.

"Did you go to Nevada at the suggestion of Perry Mason?"

She glanced in a bewildered manner toward Perry Mason.

Mason said, "I am also going to instruct the witness not to answer that question upon the ground of her constitutional rights, but, for the benefit of Court and Counsel, I will state that I am the one who suggested this young lady go to Reno, and that I paid her fare to Reno."

Had the district attorney been struck across the face with a wet towel, he could not have shown greater surprise.

"You *what?*" he asked.

"Paid this young lady's fare to Reno, and suggested that she go there," Perry Mason said. "Also, I paid her expenses while she was there."

"And you're appearing as attorney for this young woman?" Burger asked.

"Yes."

"And you refuse to allow her to answer any questions?"

"I refuse to allow her to answer the questions which you

have so far asked, and I do not think I will allow her to answer any questions you may ask."

Burger faced the witness again.

"How long have you known Richard Basset?" he asked.

"Refuse to answer that question," Mason said, "upon the ground that the answer may incriminate you."

Judge Winters leaned forward to stare down at Perry Mason.

"Counselor," he said, "the Court is beginning to believe that you are instructing this witness not to answer questions upon the ground that the answers may incriminate her, not because you feel the answers actually may incriminate *her*, but because you feel that the answers may incriminate *you*. The Court is going to give you an opportunity to be heard upon that subject and, if it appears that such is the case, the Court is going to take drastic steps."

"I am to be given an opportunity to be heard?" Perry Mason asked.

"Yes. Certainly," Judge Winters remarked with dignity.

"Very well," Perry Mason said; "under those circumstances, it becomes necessary for me to make a statement which I hoped I would not have to make.

"On the night Hartley Basset was murdered, a young woman was waiting in one of the outer offices. While she was waiting there, and at a time which was apparently immediately after the murder had been committed, a man appeared in the room. His face was covered with a mask made from carbon paper. Two eye holes had been torn in this mask. Through one of these eye holes was visible an empty eye socket."

Judge Winters said sharply, "Counselor, has this anything to do with this young woman, or her reason for not answering questions?"

Perry Mason said frankly, "Your Honor, that is not the question. The question is why I am advising this young woman not to answer questions. I am about to answer that point, and I can assure your Honor that when I have finished, I feel certain your Honor will see that everything I am now saying is pertinent, although some of it may perhaps be argumentative."

"Very well," Judge Winters remarked; "go ahead."

"The young woman screamed. The man struck at her. She tore at the mask and ripped it off. She was able to see his features. Because of a peculiar lighting arrangement, the man couldn't see her features. He struck at her again, knocked her unconscious, and probably thought he had killed her. Then he fled. Now, your Honor, that young woman is the only living person, so far as we know, who has seen the face of the man who left that room immediately after the murder had been committed."

"Well," Judge Winters said, "your own argument convinces me, Counselor, that it is a most serious offense to try and suppress that evidence, and a doubly serious offense to spirit such a witness from the jurisdiction of the court."

"I am not discussing that point at the present time," Mason said. "I am merely explaining why I have instructed this young woman not to answer questions upon the ground that they will incriminate her."

"This," Judge Winters said, "is a most amazing situation, Counselor."

"I do not claim that it isn't," Mason remarked. "I am merely seeking to make the explanation that you said you would give me an opportunity to make."

"Very well. Go ahead and make it."

"It will be obvious," Perry Mason said, "that the mask was rather an extemporaneous affair. The man who entered Basset's room came prepared to do murder. He came prepared to shoot, and yet had taken precautions so that the gun wouldn't make a noise which would be heard. In other words, he had the gun concealed under a blanket and a quilt, which served the double purpose of concealing the weapon from his victim, and also muffling the noise of the shot. That shows premeditation. He must also have prepared, in advance, a typewritten suicide note to leave in Basset's typewriter."

"You are now," Judge Winters said, frowning, "arguing against your client in the murder case."

Perry Mason's voice remained urbane.

"I am now, your Honor, patiently trying to make the explanation which you requested of me, the explanation of my position in refusing to allow this young woman to answer questions."

"But you are violating legal ethics in turning against the client whom you are representing in the murder case."

"I don't need this Court," Perry Mason said, "to instruct me as to the ethics of my profession or my duties to my client."

"Very well," Judge Winters remarked, his face turning several shades darker, "go ahead with your explanation, and be brief. Unless it is satisfactory, you will be held in contempt."

"Unfortunately," Mason said, "the explanation must be complete in order to be any explanation at all. I am calling the Court's attention to several significant details. One of these is that, had the man planned to leave by the outer office after the murder had been committed, he would have prepared his mask in advance. The *crime* shows premeditation. The *escape* does not. The mask was hastily constructed. It was constructed from materials which lay to his hand after the murder had been committed.

"Now then, your Honor, it is my contention that this whole plan of escape, this plan of exhibiting a masked face with one eye socket, was hatched in the brain of the murderer *after* the murder had been committed, for the simple reason that after the murder had been committed he recognized the potential significance of the glass eye which the victim was holding in his hand.

"It is obviously impossible that this glass eye should have dropped accidentally from the murderer's eye socket, or that it could have been grabbed by Basset during a struggle. A glass eye must be deliberately removed if it is a well-fitted glass eye. This was a well-fitted glass eye. Therefore, *why* should the murderer have deliberately removed his glass eye and deliberately exhibited the empty eye socket to a witness? There is only one reason, your Honor, and that is that the murderer felt certain no one knew about his artificial eye, but that he knew one of the suspects who would be questioned by the police did have an artificial eye, and probably suspected that the glass eye which the dead man held in his hand was the property of this suspect."

"All of this," Judge Winters said impatiently, "is merely argumentative. It is the type of argument you would make to the Court to keep your clients from being bound over. Although, I may say, Counselor, that your comments about deliberation and premeditation on the part of the murderer go far toward influencing this Court in favor of the prosecution, you are not confining yourself to the explanation which you were called upon to make. You are merely arguing."

Perry Mason bowed slightly and said, "I was about to state that when this young woman, who was the only one who could identify this man, arose from her couch, she staggered against a door and flung up her hands to brace herself. Her hands pressed against a piece of plate glass in the doorway. It occurred to me that this young woman had, therefore, left a set of finger-prints. Acting under my instructions, detectives developed those latent finger-prints, and they were classified.

"A classification of those finger-prints showed that the young woman in question is very much wanted by the police as a female Bluebeard. She's been in the habit of marrying husbands, and the husbands have developed a habit of dying within a few weeks or a few months after the marriage. In every such instance the woman has inherited property and has gone on to another marriage."

Judge Winters stared at Perry Mason in shocked, incredulous silence. Burger, the district attorney, slowly sat down, took a few deep breaths, then as slowly got to his feet. His eyes were wide with astonishment.

"We find," Perry Mason went on urbanely, "that the police have developed several cases to a point where they can virtually prove murder. This young woman secretly married Richard Basset. That marriage was bigamous. She had one husband living—that is, she had at least one husband living, probably others. The reason this particular husband was left alive was that he had lied to her about his property when he married her, and had refused to take out any insurance in her favor. Therefore, he wasn't worth killing.

"I have the proof of all of these matters. I have in this envelope a complete set of documents giving the criminal record of the young lady in question. It gives me great pleasure to hand these documents, together with photographic copies of the finger-prints left on the plate glass of the doorway, to the Prosecutor in this action.

"Now, then, your Honor, I defy even the Prosecutor in this case to intimate that in advising this woman not to answer questions upon the ground that the answers will tend to incriminate her, I have not exercised my rights as an attorney."

Burger took the envelope which Perry Mason handed him. His fingers were awkward, so great was his surprise.

Judge Winters stroked his chin for a moment, then said slowly, "Counselor, this Court has never heard such an astounding statement coming from the lips of an attorney, betraying the interest of a client whom he is supposed to represent. The Court simply cannot understand such a statement. The Court appreciates, of course, that some of your remarks consist of facts which you have learned and which probably it is your duty to communicate to the officers, but the manner in which this statement has been made, the phraseology in which it has been couched, and the time at which it was made, all tend to militate against this young woman's interests. And yet you are appearing as her attorney."

Perry Mason nodded, and said, almost casually, "Naturally, your Honor, I didn't want to make the statement, and wouldn't have done it unless the Court had forced me to do so, but you insisted that I was advising this young woman not to answer questions upon the ground that the answers would incriminate her, merely because I wanted to protect myself instead of her. I think your Honor will now see that I knew what I was doing."

Judge Winters started to say something, but he was interrupted by Burger, who lunged to his feet, holding in his right hand a photograph of a woman's full face and profile, below which appeared a printed description and a set of finger-prints.

He held in his other hand a photographic print of a set of finger-prints. He shook both papers at Perry Mason.

"Are these," he demanded of Perry Mason, "the finger-prints that were left on that doorway?"

"That is a photograph of the finger-prints, yes."

"And, do they correspond identically with the finger-prints appearing on this document which I hold in my right hand?"

"They do," Mason said.

"Then," shouted Burger, shaking the paper at Perry Mason, "some hocus-pocus has been practiced here, because the photograph of this female Bluebeard isn't the photograph of this young woman at all!"

Perry Mason smiled serenely at him.

"That," he said, "is something you can tell the Grand Jury."

Pandemonium broke loose in the courtroom.

17

JUDGE WINTERS TRIED FOR THREE MINUTES TO RESTORE ORDER in the court, and failed. He finally took a ten-minute recess and ordered bailiffs to clear the courtroom.

A bailiff appeared at Mason's elbow.

"Judge Winters would like to see you and the district attorney in his chambers," the bailiff said.

Mason nodded, accompanied the bailiff to the Judge's chambers. A moment later, the district attorney entered.

Burger glowered across at Mason and became frigidly dignified. "You wish to see me, Judge?" he asked.

"I want to discuss the very peculiar development of this situation with you gentlemen," he said.

"I have nothing whatever to discuss with Perry Mason,"

Burger announced. "Whether this woman is or is not Hazel Fenwick has nothing to do with Perry Mason's appearance before the Grand Jury."

There was a knock at the door.

"Come in," Burger called.

Judge Winters looked up in frowning annoyance. The door pushed open, and Sergeant Holcomb entered the room.

"You'll pardon me for taking liberties, Judge," Burger said, "but, under the circumstances, I have asked Sergeant Holcomb to place Perry Mason in custody."

"Custody for what?" Mason asked.

"Tampering with witnesses," Burger snapped.

"But she wasn't a witness. She didn't know one single thing about the case. She hadn't even followed it in the newspapers. She was a total stranger."

"You sent her to Reno to masquerade as Hazel Fenwick, thereby assisting the real Hazel Fenwick to escape."

"I did nothing of the sort. Hazel Fenwick had already made her escape before I even met Thelma Bevins. In view of the information I gave you in court, it should be very apparent why Hazel Fenwick had concealed herself. Doubtless the police will apprehend her. Now that they know more about her, they will be on the watch for her.

"And, as for advising this young woman to masquerade as Hazel Fenwick, I did nothing of the sort. I sent a man to serve some papers in Reno. I sent this woman to accept service of those papers. At the time the service was made, she told the man specifically and particularly that she was not Hazel Fenwick, that her name was Thelma Bevins, but that she was willing to accept service of the papers.

"For reasons of my own, I desired to have it appear that service of the papers had been made in Reno, Nevada. What those reasons are can have nothing to do with this case."

"But *why* did you do it?" Judge Winters said sternly. "That's the thing I'm getting at. I don't care to discuss this matter in public until after I've talked it over with you privately. But it seems to me that you have deliberately used the whole process of this Court to make everyone in connection with this case appear ridiculous, doubtless hoping to secure some advantage. If that is true, you have been guilty of a flagrant contempt of court and I intend to fine you and imprison you."

"I have done nothing," Mason said. "I didn't bring this young woman here. In fact, under my instructions, she refused voluntarily to leave Nevada. You will doubtless find that because of connivance between the district attorney and the Nevada authorities, she was virtually forced to leave the state and come here."

"She was a vital witness. I had a court subpœna for her, and the subpœna was served on her," Burger said.

"Exactly," Mason told him. "*You* are the one that brought her here. You were the one who assumed she was Hazel Fenwick. I didn't bring her here. I didn't make any such assumption. I didn't put her on the stand."

"But what did you hope to gain by doing it?" Judge Winters asked. "Why did you advise her not to answer questions?"

"I'll answer that question," Perry Mason told him, "only upon condition that I may answer it fully and completely and without being interrupted."

"I make no promises," Burger said, "except that you are going before the Grand Jury and that in the meantime you are going to consider yourself in custody."

"I," Judge Winters said, "will be glad to hear your explanation. I feel that it is due me and, perhaps, is due you. You have the reputation for being a very clever and adroit attorney. There is usually some reason back of what you do. I would be glad to know what it was in this case."

"Very well, Judge," Mason said. "Everyone in this room has lost sight of the fact that there is one man who had reason to fear Hazel Fenwick more than any other mortal on earth. That man is the murderer of Hartley Basset.

"He didn't know what Hazel Fenwick looked like. Therefore, if the district attorney should produce some woman who apparently was Hazel Fenwick and put her on the stand, that man would think that the jig was up. He would naturally resort to flight.

"I think you are all overlooking the significance of my comments in court to the effect that Brunold could not have committed this crime because he would not have deliberately placed his own eye in Hartley Basset's hand after the murder had been committed. Nor, on the other hand, could the eye have been snatched from its socket by Hartley Basset, nor, even if we are to suppose that it could, would Brunold have deliberately masked the balance of his face, but left visible the empty socket, which would have been one of the most sure means of identification.

"On the other hand, if some other person in that household had an artificial eye and that fact was not suspected by any of the other persons in the house, he would have gone to great lengths to have made it appear that the crime was committed by a person who had only one eye, feeling that by so doing he was directing suspicion to Brunold.

"I tried to get photographs of every one of the persons in that house, facing a strong light. As you are doubtless aware, it is very difficult to detect an artificial eye where the eye is well made, matched and fitted, and where the socket has not in any wise been destroyed. However, a natural eye adjusts itself to light, the pupil dilating or contracting, while an artificial eye obviously cannot make such adjustments. Therefore, a person photographed facing a bright light would show pupils of unequal diameter if he had one glass eye.

"It happened that Colemar refused to pose for a photograph. That made me quite suspicious of Colemar. I am now wondering if Colemar didn't think the young woman who was placed on the stand by the district attorney was the missing witness who could positively identify him and that, as soon as the legal wrangling between counsel was over, she would unhesitatingly do so. I think, therefore, it might be well to check up upon the present whereabouts of Mr. Colemar."

At that moment the telephone rang, and Judge Winters picked up the receiver, placed it to his ear and said, "Just a moment." He nodded to Perry Mason.

"A young lady," he said, "wishes to speak with you."

Mason put the receiver to his ear and heard Della Street's voice coming over the wire.

"Cheerio, Chief," she said. "Are you still out of jail?"

He grinned into the transmitter and said, "Half and half—half in and half out."

"Well," she said, "I was just a little bit dumb. I didn't realize what you were up to with that Bevins girl until after I heard you advising her not to answer questions. Then I saw a great white light."

"Good girl," he told her.

"So," she said, "I made up my mind that I'd sort of stick around and see if any of the witnesses found occasion to leave the courtroom rather abruptly or surreptitiously."

"Good girl," he repeated. "Did you get any customers?"

"I'll say."

"Who?"

"Colemar."

"Did you tail him?"

"Yes."

"That," he told her, frowning, "was dangerous. You shouldn't have done it."

"You gave me a signal," she said. "I wasn't certain you meant everything was under control or whether you wanted me to take a tumble to your technique and trail along."

"Where is he now, Della?"

"He's at the Union Airport. A plane leaves in twenty-two minutes. He has a ticket for it."

"Be sure," he told her, "that you keep out of sight. The man's desperate."

"How's the case coming?" she asked.

"All finished," he told her. "You beat it up to the office. I'll meet you there."

"I want to see this thing through," she said. "You wait there in the Judge's chambers and let me call you if he takes another run-out powder."

"I don't want you hanging around. He may recognize you at any time and . . ."

She laughed lightly, and said, "Cheerio, Chief," and hung up.

Perry Mason consulted his wrist watch and looked at Sergeant Holcomb.

"It may interest you gentlemen to know that Colemar is at the Union Airport and will be there for approximately twenty-one minutes. It occurs to me, Sergeant, that if you made certain your gun was loaded you *might* make a rather spectacular arrest."

Holcomb looked at Burger. Burger frowned thoughtfully, then nodded his head. Sergeant Holcomb gained the door in three swift strides. Perry Mason, lounging on the arm of the chair, grinned across at Burger.

"Mason," the district attorney asked, somewhat sheepishly, "why the devil did you put on all that horse play?"

"It wasn't horse play," Mason insisted. "I ran into a bum break, that's all. The witness who could have cleared my client was wanted by the cops. She had to take a run-out powder. Naturally, I got the credit for her disappearance and it left my clients in a spot. I could probably have trapped Colemar on cross-examination, but I wanted as many strings to my bow as I could get. So I tried this stunt. I knew that if I could make him think the Fenwick woman had been returned and was going to be a witness against him he'd either have to kill her or resort to flight. He couldn't very well have killed her while she was in a courtroom surrounded by officers. So I put on an act to make him think the jig was up, but that he was going to have a few hours of grace while a bunch of lawyers were wrangling back and forth. I figured he thought I really had spirited the girl away and that it would take a Grand Jury hearing to make her talk. That would give him a chance to run away."

"Would you," asked Judge Winters, "mind explaining to me exactly what happened? I find myself very much in the dark."

Mason nodded. "Colemar," he said, "was the partner of Harry McLane in an embezzlement. They embezzled money from Basset. Brunold was the father of Mrs. Basset's child. He'd spent years hunting for her after she had disappeared.

When he found her, she was married. He called on her. The chauffeur, who was acting for Basset as spy, almost caught him. Brunold wanted her to leave Basset. She wasn't decided as to what she was going to do, but she did know that if Hartley Basset ever caught Brunold in her room, he would make a terrific scandal which would affect the boy. That was one of the things she didn't want. So she spirited Brunold out of the room. He dropped his glass eye when he was getting out—not the one he was wearing, but an extra one he carried in his pocket.

"Basset got that glass eye. He didn't know the identity of his wife's visitor, but he *did* know that Colemar had a glass eye. Apparently, he was the only one in the house who knew it. The eyes are pretty much the same color, if you'll notice. Basset got suspicious of Colemar, suspecting him of being intimate with his wife—something of which Colemar was entirely innocent. But, when Basset started checking up on Colemar, he uncovered evidence of Colemar's part in the embezzlement.

"Harry McLane went out to Basset's house, not to see Basset or to pay him off, but to force Colemar to kick through with enough of the embezzled money to keep Basset from prosecuting. About that time, Brunold was out making a final appeal to Mrs. Basset to leave the place, and Dick Basset was sending his young wife down to get acquainted with her father-in-law.

"Colemar thought he could intercede for McLane, that a little conversation might save a lot of cash. Basset called him on the glass eye business, sent him, probably, for some books of account, and showed his general suspicion. Colemar didn't bring the books. He picked up a quilt, a blanket and a gun. He also typed out a suicide note. Later on he suddenly realized that he would be the person logically suspected by the police if they weren't fooled by the suicide note—that was after the murder had been committed. So he cleaned the forged notes out of the file, extemporized a mask out of some carbon paper and ran out to show the woman who was waiting in the outer office that the murderer was a one-eyed man.

He figured that would tie in nicely with the glass eye which Basset still held in his hand. When the woman surprised him by ripping off the mask, he was in a frenzy of panic. He struck her down and ran out of the place. He jumped in Basset's car, drove it away, then circled back to the garage, put up the car, came back and pretended he'd been to a movie. He found out then that he hadn't killed the Fenwick woman. He wanted to silence her forever. So he entered the room where the Fenwick girl was and kept hanging around. If he'd been left alone with her, he'd have killed her, but Mrs. Basset sent him out. Then he went up to his room and explained to McLane what had happened and that all McLane had to do was to insist he'd paid off the notes and no one could prove differently. That would have made it appear Basset had a lot of cash on him at the time of the murder and make the motive look like robbery."

Burger, staring at Perry Mason, said, "How do *you* know all this?"

"Simply by deductive reasoning," Mason said. "My God, Burger, it stuck out so plainly that it's a wonder it needed anyone to point it out to you. The murder *must* have been committed by a professional typist. The fake suicide note was written by a professional typist, someone who used the touch system. The murderer must also have been someone who was able to walk into Basset's study carrying something on his arm without attracting undue attention, because Basset didn't put up any fight, apparently hadn't sensed any danger. The murderer must have been someone with an artificial eye who wanted the authorities to know that he had an artificial eye. The only possible reason that a person would want to advertise his artificial eye was that he felt suspicion could thereby be directed on someone else.

"Moreover, Mrs. Basset wanted the Fenwick girl to have an uninterrupted interview with Hartley Basset. Therefore, she watched the front door until the last client had left before taking the Fenwick woman down to Hartley Basset's outer office. Yet, when this woman knocked at the door of Basset's inner office, some man was in there talking with Basset. That man must have been Colemar, unless it was someone who had entered through the back door, which wasn't very likely.

"Moreover, *if* a one-eyed man had been making a mask very hurriedly only for the purpose of concealing his features, he would only have torn out *one* eye hole. The fact that he tore out *two* eye holes shows that he was trying to direct attention to the empty eye socket. Now, if that had been Brunold, he'd never have advertised the fact of that empty eye socket."

"Then," Burger said, "young McLane must have been killed because he was going to talk."

"Probably," Mason said.

"But why the devil did the person who killed young McLane put a glass eye in his palm? That must have been done by Colemar. *Why* did he do it?"

Perry Mason, looking very innocent, said, "After all, Burger, there's only so much one can accomplish by using deductive reasoning. I'm free to confess that I'm at the end of my rope. I can't give you an answer to that."

Burger stared at him steadily. Mason, his face perfectly composed, puffed placidly at his cigarette.

Judge Winters slowly nodded his head. "Obvious," he said, "from the beginning, if a person hadn't allowed his mind to be blinded by a lot of extraneous details and had concentrated upon the obvious."

Perry Mason stretched and yawned, looked at his wrist watch and said, "I'd certainly like to hear from Sergeant Holcomb. I hope he gets Colemar without a shooting."

Burger said slowly, "Mason, you should have been a detective instead of a lawyer."

"Thank you," Mason told him. "I'm doing very well as it is."

"How did you know I was going to fall for the Bevins woman and bring her into court?" Burger asked.

"Because," Mason told him, "I'm too old a campaigner to underestimate an adversary. I knew that you'd get her here some way. I timed the whole play so that you would just about have time to bring her in as a surprise witness and confound me with her. I figured you'd do that."

"But you didn't tell her anything of your plans?"

"No, I figured the less she knew, the less she'd have to tell. I knew that if she told you folks the truth, you'd think she was lying."

"How did you know we'd be able to get her here?"

"That is where I didn't underestimate your ability, Burger."

Burger sighed, got to his feet and started pacing the floor.

"It's plain enough, now that it's pointed out," he said, "but, by God, I'd have sworn Brunold committed that murder with the connivance and assistance of Mrs. Basset, and I'd have prosecuted them and demanded the death penalty, at least for Brunold."

He dropped into a chair and fell silent.

"After all," Judge Winters said in an aggrieved voice, "you should have taken me in on the play, Counselor, so that I wouldn't have appeared so ridiculous there in the courtroom."

Mason smiled, and said, "You'll pardon me, your Honor, and understand that the remark contains nothing of disrespect, but if you hadn't appeared so ridiculous, as you term it, you wouldn't have appeared convincing."

For a moment Judge Winters' forehead came together in a frown, then the corners of his lips tilted.

"Oh, well," he said, "have it your own way."

Perry Mason pinched out his cigarette end, looked at his wrist watch, and lit another cigarette. Burger turned to Mason and said, "How the devil am I going to square myself with the newspapers?"

Mason waved his hand in a generous gesture.

"Take it all," he said.

"All of what?"

"All of the credit. Figure that it was an act you put on with me for the purpose of trapping the real murderer."

A gleam of quick interest showed in Burger's eyes.

Abruptly the door burst open. Three newspaper men came storming into the room. They descended upon Burger with a barrage of questions.

"Wait a minute," Burger said. "What's happened?"

"Out at the airport—a shooting. Sergeant Holcomb's

wounded, and Colemar killed. How did Colemar get out there? What was he doing? Why did Sergeant Holcomb go after him?"

One of the news men detached himself from the others, grabbed Mason's arm.

"What about it, Mason?" he shouted. "Give us the low-down. It's the biggest thing you've ever pulled. . . ."

Perry Mason sighed.

"Mr. Burger," he said, "will make the statement to the press in our joint behalf. In the meantime, gentlemen, if you'll pardon me, I've got to go to my office."

18

PERRY MASON LEANED BACK IN HIS OFFICE CHAIR. THE TOP of his desk was littered with newspapers.

"Good for Sergeant Holcomb," he said. "I always knew he had the stuff in him."

"I thought you hated him," Della Street remarked.

"His stupidity is irritating at times," Mason agreed, "but it's only because of his zeal that he gets himself into those situations. So Colemar pulled a gun and tried to smoke his way out when he saw he was cornered?"

She nodded slowly.

"In many ways," Mason said, "that last situation is typical of the pair of them. Sergeant Holcomb came roaring up to the airport with his sirens screaming."

"But he had to use his siren to make the time he did through traffic," Della Street pointed out.

"Certainly, through traffic. But not *after* he had gone through the traffic. He had the whole airport in front of him, and yet he had to come up with his sirens screaming. Of course Colemar knew what that meant. He hid in the Men's Room, put his eye to the keyhole and waited to see what happened. After a while, Holcomb started for the restroom. Colemar poked his gun through the glass panel in the door and opened fire. If he hadn't been nervous, he'd have killed Holcomb with that first shot.

"So far, Holcomb had run true to form. He blundered everything he did. He alarmed his quarry by going up to the station with the siren going. He should have known, after he had searched the waiting room, that Colemar was in the Men's Room. The fact that he suspected it strongly is indicated by the fact that he strode toward the door. A more intelligent man would have moved up on the place from the side, jerked the door open, leveled his gun, and ordered his prisoner to come out. But not Holcomb. He pounded up toward the door, broadside on. Then comes the side of Sergeant Holcomb that gets my respect and admiration.

"That was a .45 slug that hit him in the shoulder. And, sister, I'm here to tell you that a .45 slug, catching a man in the shoulder, takes a lot of steam out of him. Holcomb didn't even have his gun in his hand."

She nodded.

"Tell me," he asked, "did he stop while he was getting his gun out, or what did he do?"

"He kept right on walking," she said. "The impact of that slug turned him halfway around. He straightened himself, set his jaw, and kept walking toward that door, pulling out his gun as he walked. Colemar took one more shot, and Holcomb started shooting through the door. You could see the places where his slugs went through the wood. He made as perfect a group as though he'd been shooting at a target on the police range."

Mason nodded slowly, and said, "A damn good man. It takes guts to do that."

Mason picked up one of the newspapers. District Attorney Burger's likeness was spread over three columns on the front page. Below it, in large print, appeared:

FIGHTING DISTRICT ATTORNEY WHO CLEVERLY
TRAPPED THE SLAYER OF HARTLEY BASSET
INTO BETRAYING HIMSELF

To the right, and slightly below, was a picture of Sergeant Holcomb. The space in between was filled with line drawings showing Sergeant Holcomb approaching the door of the Men's Room, firing from the hip, while Colemar was crouched back of the door, emptying a .45 revolver at the officer.

"They certainly hogged plenty of credit," Della Street said resentfully, her voice betraying her feelings. "You were the one who thought it all out. You put the cards in their hands. All *they* had to do was to lay them down and take the tricks."

Mason chuckled.

"You saw that Thelma Bevins got her money?" he asked.

"Yes. And she got a nice bonus from Pete Brunold."

"Good for Brunold. He's great stuff for the sob-sisters, isn't he? . . . Thelma Bevins came through splendidly."

"What would you have done, Chief, if she'd fallen down? She could have become frightened, you know, and told the whole story before she got on the witness stand."

"The nice part of it was," Mason said, "that she couldn't. If she told Burger the story of what actually had happened, Burger would have become convinced she was a clever liar and was simply trying to protect me. Using the build-up that I did, Burger hypnotized himself on her identity. And the more she denied it, the more he'd have become certain she was lying."

"But suppose something *had* happened?"

"I could have blasted it out of Colemar," he said slowly, "on cross-examination. But I didn't want to do it."

"Why?"

"Because then it would have looked as though I'd slipped one over on Burger. Burger gave me a square deal. I wanted to give him one. Burger has a horror of prosecuting an innocent man. That's a distinct asset so far as I'm concerned. Looking back on this case, his recollections are going to be very pleasant. He'll give me the breaks the next time I want him to investigate some particular piece of evidence."

"Chief," she said suddenly, "how *did* that glass eye get put into Harry McLane's hand? It's certain Colemar wouldn't have put it there."

Mason looked at her and smiled significantly.

The meaning of that smile dawned upon her.

"Why," she exclaimed, "you . . . you could have . . . !"

"It would," Mason said, "have been a swell break for Brunold, *if* Brunold had been in jail at the time the murder was committed. Unfortunately, he wasn't. I had to move fast to keep the police from suspecting him."

"But you shouldn't have done that. In the first place, you had no right taking those chances. In the second place it wasn't . . . wasn't . . . I can't describe it."

"Is ethical the word you're groping for?" he asked.

"Not exactly. It's so out of keeping with your position. You do the darnedest things. You're half saint and half devil. There isn't any middle ground. You go to both extremes."

He laughed at her and said, "I hate mediocrity."

"How about Hazel Fenwick?" she asked.

"They'll pick her up one of these days," Mason told her. "Dick Basset certainly had a narrow escape. If it hadn't been for that murder, the female Bluebeard would have chalked up two more victims."

"*Two* more!"

"Sure," he said. "She'd have bumped Hartley Basset first, and then Dick. Perhaps she'd have cleaned up on Sylvia Basset as well."

"How can women do things like that?"

"Just sort of a disease," he said. "It's a mental quirk."

THE PERRY MASON MYSTERIES by

Erle Stanley Gardner
Investigate 'em!